*Yo...*

Tale... ...arlequin Blaze author Debbi Rawlins makes all your cowboy dreams come true with her popular miniseries

**Made in Montana**

The little town of Blackfoot Falls isn't so sleepy anymore...

In fact, it seems everyone's staying up late!

Get your hands on a hot cowboy with

**#837 *Anywhere with You***
(March 2015)

**#849 *Come On Over***
(June 2015)

**#861 *This Kiss***
(September 2015)

*And remember, the sexiest cowboys are Made in Montana!*

Dear Reader,

I've been living in a small rural town for almost a decade now and I must say it's been quite a learning experience. Often it's been fun, certainly surprising. And, admittedly, I do a fair bit of eye-rolling. Best thing about living here, though? It's been great inspiration for the fictional town of Blackfoot Falls in my Made in Montana series.

Yes, I've shamelessly eavesdropped while getting my hair cut, grabbing lunch at the local diner or waiting in line at the post office. With so many of the ranches passed down from one generation to the next, there always seems to be an interesting story or piece of gossip surrounding the families who first settled here a hundred and fifty years ago. It got me wondering about the legal aspect of passing down land and livestock. Are things made nice and tidy via a will? Or is an assumption enough? Or maybe a handshake?

In *Come On Over*, the Eager Beaver Ranch arose from my latest "what if" game. You'll meet Trent and Shelby, two characters who were a pleasure for me to write, especially since they did all the heavy lifting...

Thanks so much for visiting me and the folks of Blackfoot Falls!

Debbi Rawlins

# Debbi Rawlins

## Come On Over

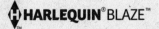
HARLEQUIN® BLAZE™

Recycling programs
for this product may
not exist in your area.

ISBN-13: 978-0-373-79853-7

Come On Over

Copyright © 2015 by Debbi Quattrone

**Printed in U.S.A.**

www.Harlequin.com

**Debbi Rawlins** grew up in the country and loved Westerns in movies and books. Her first crush was on a cowboy—okay, he was an actor in the role of a cowboy, but she was only eleven, so it counts. It was in Houston, Texas, where she first started writing for Harlequin, and now she has her own ranch...of sorts. Instead of horses, she has four dogs, four cats, a trio of goats and free-range cattle on a few acres in gorgeous rural Utah.

### Books by Debbi Rawlins

#### HARLEQUIN BLAZE

##### *Made in Montana*

*Barefoot Blue Jean Night*
*Own the Night*
*On a Snowy Christmas Night*
*You're Still the One*
*No One Needs to Know*
*From This Moment On*
*Alone with You*
*Need You Now*
*Behind Closed Doors*
*Anywhere with You*

To get the inside scoop on Harlequin Blaze and its talented writers, be sure to check out blazeauthors.com.

All backlist available in ebook format.

Visit the Author Profile page at Harlequin.com for more titles.

## _1_

THE EAGER BEAVER was cursed. Trent Kimball had always been a skeptic, but right now, trying to get this damned old tractor to run, he was tempted to rethink his position.

His dad had moved the whole family off the ranch when Trent was sixteen, swearing by the words of Trent's great-granddad that anyone who tried to make something of the place was doomed to failure.

Three years later Trent's older brother had tried to give it a go but after seven years, he'd gone belly up. When Colby had blamed it on the curse, Trent had given him a load of crap about superstition and other nonsense.

In truth, if his bottom-feeding, soul-sucking ex-wife hadn't damn near cleaned him out, Trent wouldn't be here trying to whip the ranch into shape. But cursed? Nah, when it came right down to it, he wasn't about to jinx his future when he'd barely gotten started. Eight months was nothing when it came to building a new life.

Using a clean rag to wipe the sweat off his forehead, he squinted at the gap in the east corral where a pair of rails had come loose and fallen during the night. He'd get to that later today. The job he was on right now was far more urgent. He stared at the tractor engine. If he didn't get it running soon, he was gonna be in a world of hurt. Alfalfa wasn't cheap. He needed to be ready to plant come spring. And after building the stable his bank account was dwindling fast. He jerked the wrench. And caught the edge of his thumb.

He let loose a string of cussing everyone in Blackfoot Falls, sixteen miles away, must've heard. Mutt didn't even raise his head. The mangy hound stayed put, a huge lump of black fur curled up under the shade of a cottonwood. Damn lazy dog.

Violet, his unwelcome neighbor, didn't miss her chance to mock him and she sure as hell didn't hold back. The unseasonably warm fall breeze carried the sound of her cackling straight to him. He turned to the wiry old woman sitting on the porch of her double-wide parked near the faded barn. As usual she was smoking an oversize pipe and having a fine time in her dilapidated oak rocker.

One of these days she'd end up on her butt. Twice he'd offered to fix the chair for her. *Twice*. But as she so bluntly put it…his carpentry skills sucked. Much as he hated to admit it, she had a point.

Though he was getting better. He'd done a meticulous job of finishing the inside of the stable himself, making sure it was hazard-free, before he'd brought Solomon and Jax, a pair of quarter horses he'd purchased a couple of years back.

Still, the laughter coming off the porch was frying his nerves to a crisp. Here he'd cleaned her gutters, repaired the stairs by her front door and built her a handrail. But had she thanked him?

Okay, so he'd done those things when Violet was off to town so she wouldn't give him any lip. And yes, the woman was a burr in his boot, but he didn't want her hurt. Just quiet. And minding her own business.

"I know you have an air conditioner and a TV inside,

Violet Merriweather," he said, taking off his hat then re-settling it on his head. "Why the hell are you sitting out here in the heat watching me?"

"You're funnier than any of them reality shows." She might've grinned, hard to tell with the pipe hiding half her craggy features. "Anyhow, I'm all caught up on *Duck Dynasty*."

Trent sighed. If he had any sense he would've run her off the property when he'd first returned to Montana. The old woman had a knack for making him feel like a complete loser, and that was the last thing he needed right now. But she had no kids, no family since her brother had passed away some years back, and she'd watched him and Colby grow up. Over the years, Violet had become a fixture at the ranch. But they'd both been nicer then.

Somewhere in her mid-eighties, she was still spry and wiry, and had plenty of opinions she was more than willing to share. For all he knew, being cantankerous was the secret to staying young.

A stiff crosswind out of the west brought the aroma of baked beans and cornbread. Had to be coming from Violet's stove. Their closest neighbor lived three miles away. Another whiff and Trent's stomach growled loud enough for Mutt to lift his head. Or maybe it was the smell that roused the dog's attention. His eyes looked mighty hopeful.

"You think that's coming from our kitchen?" Trent snorted. "Dream on."

Mutt let out a huff.

"You know as well as I do she won't share." Which was a shame. Anything beyond frying eggs and bacon tested his kitchen skills. He'd offered to pay Violet to cook for him, but she'd turned him down flat. "Don't look at me like that," he told Mutt who'd let out a whine. "You eat better than I do."

The dog had shown up the day Trent arrived. Halfway

down the gravel driveway, he'd noticed Mutt trotting behind the U-Haul he had towed all the way from Texas.
Most of the stuff he cared about probably could've fit in
the back of his truck. But he'd jam-packed the small rental
with a few chairs, an end table, his favorite couch, the king-
size bed he and Dana had shared and a few other things he
didn't particularly want, but damned if he'd let her have
them. He'd been too angry to see anything but red.

Two days after the race that'd had him and everyone
else in the racing world questioning his ability as a horse
trainer, she'd walked into their bedroom with an empty
suitcase and handed it to him. Told him she wanted a divorce. Just like that. How had he not seen that side of her
before? They'd married too young, still in the giddy stage
of love and lust when they'd eloped without a word to anyone. And in the three years they were together, he'd seen
her angry, hurt, pouty, even spiteful at times, but to kick
a man when he was already down?

Clearly he'd underestimated Dana's need to have a
wealthy, successful husband. She'd given up on him before the dust had even settled. Her lack of confidence in
his ability to train more winning horses, making the big
bucks she'd never had trouble spending, had taken a chunk
of his heart. That last race, that one missed call, couldn't
have been the only straw. But he'd had no idea it would
be the last.

As for their divorce settlement, he figured giving her the
big house and fancy sports car he'd paid for with his bonus
money was more than enough. Hell, he'd never wanted the
big colonial anyway. Or the car for that matter.

Mutt turned toward the driveway. The dog was smart,
probably half border collie, and at least five years old. Poor
guy was on the homely side, with one brown eye and the
other a spooky gold. It had taken two baths before Trent
was able to tell Mutt's chest was gray.

When he let out a long, low growl, Trent shaded his eyes and peered toward the road. He didn't get many visitors, and certainly none driving black luxury sedans.

"It's okay, boy." Trent bent to stroke the dog's side, but kept his gaze on the car as it turned down the long driveway. He glanced at Violet. "You expecting anyone?"

"What do you think?" she muttered, her frown aimed at the slowly approaching vehicle.

Right, silly question. "Sit," he told Mutt, and the dog promptly obeyed. "Stay." As the car neared the barn, Trent tugged down the rim of his hat to block the afternoon sun and started walking.

The tinted windows wouldn't let him see the driver but he noticed the Colorado plates. Whoever it was had to be lost. Not many people came out this far. After idling for a bit, the engine was cut. Trent stood near the hood on the passenger side, dusting off the front of his jeans while he waited for the driver's door to open.

A few seconds later a woman stepped out. The breeze whipped long strands of honey-blond hair across her face, preventing Trent from getting a good look at her. With a delicate hand she swept the hair out of her eyes.

She blinked at him, then smiled. "Hello."

"Afternoon," he said, touching the brim of his hat. She was pretty. Real pretty. High cheekbones. Full mouth. "Can I help you?"

"I hope so." She glanced at the small brick house. "I think this is the Eager Beaver ranch? The sign on the post is really faded."

"Yeah, um…" Trying not to grimace, he rubbed the back of his neck. Only the word Beaver was left on the wooden sign. He'd kinda thought it was funny. Until now. "I've been meaning to get around to that."

"Oh?" Her brows rose. She blinked again, looking confused as she scanned the rundown barn, sheds and chicken coop. When she lifted a hand and smiled, he saw Violet leaning forward. "I'm sorry," the woman said. "Please excuse my bad manners. I'm Shelby." She came around the hood, one hand extended, the other busy trying to keep from being blinded by the breeze tangling her hair. "Shelby Foster."

"Trent—" His fingers grazed hers. He yanked his hand back just in time. Grease and dirt streaked his palm. "Sorry, I've been working on the tractor."

She smelled good, sweet. Not perfumy, but more like the first clean whiff of spring. And her eyes, they were green. Like fresh-cut hay. When she narrowed them he realized he was staring like a jackass.

"Okay," she said. "I'm not sure I understand. If this is the Eager Beaver, you must be—" Her worried gaze darted to the equipment shed, then back to the house. "So, are you the—caretaker?"

"If I were, I'd be doing a mighty sorry job of it," he said with a laugh.

"Whew." Shelby grinned. "That's what I was thinking."

"Wait a minute—" His indignation only lasted a second. But then he got so distracted by her long slender legs, he forgot what he was about to say. "Who are you again?"

"Shelby Foster."

"No. I mean why are you here?"

"Well…" With a tentative smile she glanced at the porch that needed repairing. "I'm the new owner."

He pushed up the brim of his hat as if that would improve his hearing. "Come again?"

"Okay, not *new*. Actually it's been a year. But this is the first time I've come to see the place for myself."

Trent studied her face, the overly bright smile, the uncertainty in her eyes as her gaze swept toward the barn. It didn't seem as if she was joking and somehow he didn't think she was crazy.

"Who put you up to this?" he asked, closely watching her reaction. "Was it Colby?"

Her puzzled frown seemed genuine. "Put me up to what?"

"I know you're not the owner because I am."

Shelby raised her eyebrows. "You can't be."

"Yes, ma'am, I can." He removed his Stetson and shoved a hand through his hair, damp from sweat and starting to curl at his nape. He jammed the hat back on. "This ranch has been in my family for four generations."

"I don't understand," she said, a flicker of panic in her eyes. "How is that possible?"

Trent sure hoped she wasn't a victim of one of those auction scams. Buy property sight-unseen for cheap, then find out the paperwork is fake. The car, the clothes screamed success. She didn't look like someone who'd be that foolish. "There are a whole bunch of ranches around Blackfoot Falls. Maybe you got confused?"

"Any of them named the Eager Beaver?"

At her insulting tone of voice, any sympathy he'd felt for her dimmed. He liked the name, dammit. "Let's back up here. What makes you think you own the place?"

"I have the deed."

"The what?"

"The deed…it's a legal document—"

"I know what a deed is," he said, cutting her off. Hell, did she think he was some hayseed? Which brought to mind… "You don't look like a rancher or an outdoor kind of gal." He'd started his inspection with her fine leather boots, probably perfect for a night in the city but not out here. Her designer jeans could go either way, he supposed. But her clingy blue top? And those full pink lips…

He finally met her eyes. An icy chill darkened them and dared him to say another word. Or take another look.

Trent just smiled. She was safe from him. He was done with women, but looking was an entirely different matter.

From his kitchen window, he loved watching the sun dip behind the Rockies. Didn't mean he planned on climbing them.

Lifting her chin, she said, "Now that we've established I'm the owner, who are you?"

"We what?" And here he'd worried she might be the victim of a con. Jesus. She really did think he was a country bumpkin. "You have a deed? I'd like to see it."

Her confidence faltered. Or maybe swiping her tongue across her lips was supposed to distract him. It almost worked. "I don't have it with me," she said, taking a deep breath that made her chest rise. "It's with my things, which will be arriving next week."

"Your things?" He stared at her, and she nodded. "No. No way. You call whoever's hauling your stuff and—" From his peripheral vision, he noticed Violet edging closer. He didn't need her sticking her nose in this. "Let's go in the house," he told Shelby in a more reasonable tone. "We can get something cold to drink. Figure this thing out."

She moistened her lips again, her expression cautious as she inspected his stained brown T-shirt, worn jeans and dusty boots.

"I'm not gonna bite," he said when she didn't move.

"Fine." With a toss of her hair, she picked her way through the gravel to the porch steps, having some trouble with those skinny, impractical boot heels.

He followed behind, torn between checking out her shapely rear end and keeping an eye on Violet. It would be just like her to stir up trouble, for sheer sport if nothing else. When he saw the old busybody closing the distance between them, he whistled for Mutt to run interference. At best, Trent had a fifty-fifty shot the dog would listen.

Shelby stopped at the screen door and turned to him.

"Go on inside. It's not locked."

She glanced past him, then entered the house.

He caught the screen and smiled when he saw that Mutt was doing his job. Violet stood near the barn, spewing curses and trying to evade the dog's long eager tongue. She liked the mooch well enough, even slipped him treats, but she couldn't stand him licking her.

"Come on, boy." Trent waited for the dog to bound up the steps and charge inside.

Yanking off his hat, he walked into the living room. Looking terrified, Shelby stood frozen, against the far wall where Mutt had cornered her. Jesus, he hadn't considered...

"Come," Trent commanded, but Mutt ignored him.

SHELBY FIGURED IF the dog was going to bite her, he'd have already done so. She tucked her purse under her arm, and crouched to pet the big shaggy fur ball that had to be over sixty pounds. She loved dogs but couldn't for the life of her identify his breed.

"Well, aren't you a cutie pie trying to look all ferocious." She found his sweet spot—a patch low behind his ear—and lightly raked it with her nails until his big eyes rolled back in contentment. "He has mud on his paws," she said, eyeing the dusty wood floor. "If you care."

She immediately regretted being snide. Trent ignored it, but she knew he'd heard. It wasn't like her to be rude. But she was tired, hungry and not completely enamored of the run-down Eager Beaver ranch. Stupid name, anyway. She'd look into changing it first thing.

And then there was Trent, whoever he was...besides tall and hot. Though being good-looking didn't work in his favor. Not with her. She'd had it with men. And their expectations. And...well, just about everything.

"How many times have I told you to use the doormat?" Trent said to the dog, then ducked out and returned with a faded towel. "He get any mud on you?"

She shook her head, then looked up. Trent's eyes were an unusual gray. She hadn't been able to tell earlier, but she'd noticed the strong jaw shadowed from a couple days' growth of beard. With his dark wavy hair, tanned skin and long, lean body, he was the perfect image of the untamed cowboy conquering the rugged West. If a woman had a fanciful imagination, which she did not. Anyway, she was from Colorado and knew better. Not all cowboys were equal. But all men were.

No, that wasn't fair. She looked at her left hand, where her engagement ring used to be. She was still raw from Donald's betrayal. From the proof that while he wanted to marry her, he didn't know her at all. In time the sting would fade. She had to believe that if she wanted to start fresh, prove to herself she could be successful on her own terms.

"Come here, boy." Trent crouched beside her and gave the dog's collar a light tug until his front paws were on the towel.

Huddling between Trent and a console table felt too intimate so she stood. "What's his name?"

"Mutt. Actually, it's Ugly Mutt. Sometimes I call him Ugly. But mostly just Mutt."

She stared down at him, ready and waiting to disappoint him when he looked for her reaction to his baiting. But he never looked up, simply concentrated on cleaning the dog's paws while her gaze followed the play of corded muscle along his forearms.

"You're kidding, right?" she said finally.

"About?"

"His name. You don't really call him Ugly."

"Sure I do." He gave the dog an affectionate pat. "Look at him."

"That's awful." How could he treat the poor animal that way? "*You're* awful."

Trent smiled. "You know he doesn't understand, right?"

Her gaze caught on the laugh lines fanning out at the corner of his eye. Then slid to his muscled bicep straining the sleeve of the T-shirt. When she finally noticed that he was giving her a funny look, she realized she'd stopped listening.

She cleared her throat and surveyed the room. "We need to straighten out this mess."

Trent glanced over his shoulder and frowned at the magazines and newspapers littering the coffee table. A pair of boots, one turned on its side, butted up to the burgundy recliner. "Which mess are we talking about?"

"The Eager Beaver," she said, as it slowly dawned on her that the place was furnished with chairs, a high-quality leather sofa, a flat-screen TV, rugs... Trent wasn't simply squatting or passing through. "And how quickly you can clear off my property."

He wasn't taking her one bit seriously. With a lifted brow he slid his gaze down her body. "You suddenly found that deed somewhere?"

"No. I explained where it is. But you seem so sure of yourself, I'm assuming you have one."

That wiped the smirk off his face. "I do. Not here. My folks have it in their bank safe-deposit box."

"In Blackfoot Falls? Shouldn't take you long to get it."

"They live in Dillon, four hours from here."

"Oh, how convenient."

"Says the woman who claims her papers are in transit." He pushed to his feet, bringing him a good five inches taller than her even with her three-inch heels. "What kind of—" He cut himself off, clamped his mouth shut.

They were standing too close to each other. Boxed in by the wall, table and Trent, she could feel his body heat and a hint of his breath on her cheek. Oddly, he smelled good, sort of woodsy, even though she knew he'd been working outside in the sun.

When he wouldn't move, she slipped around him. "You were saying?" she said, sneaking a peek in the bright yellow kitchen, surprised to see an open laptop sitting on a table.

"Nothing."

"Please." She turned to find him meticulously wiping his hands with the towel. "By all means, finish what you were about to say."

He looked up, his gaze narrowing.

Okay, that might've come out a bit haughty.

With his sights locked on her, he said, "I was wondering what kind of idiot packs important legal papers with their belongings instead of keeping the documents locked up or with them."

Heat surged up her neck and into her face. Someone who'd left in a hurry. Someone who'd been foolish enough to overstay where she hadn't belonged in the first place.

"I deserved that," Shelby said quietly. "I'm sorry."

His gaze lowered before he looked away. "We'll get this straightened out, but I'm warning you, it won't be the outcome you want."

She bit her lip. He seemed awfully sure, she thought, again taking in the furniture, most of it quite nice. The truth was, she didn't really have the deed in her possession, only her grandfather's will. Of course she'd call the attorney who'd drawn the will up. Something she would've already done if she hadn't been in such a rush to get away from her ex-fiancé and his family.

"You should try The Boarding House Inn in town. Better hurry, though, it's getting late and there isn't another inn for miles."

Shelby studied his expressionless face. Naturally he

was trying to get rid of her. "Hmm, I could ask around about you."

"Good idea. Most folks know me, or at least they know my family. They'll confirm what I've told you."

Her mouth went dry. Her heart sank. This wasn't looking good at all. Maybe he was bluffing.

"Hey, how about that cold drink I promised? I've got orange juice, water, beer…"

Annoyed that he must've noticed her difficulty swallowing, she shook her head. "How far is it to town?"

"Sixteen miles."

"And you don't care if I inquire about you," she said, watching him closely.

"Nope. Ask anyone."

A knock at the door had them both turning their heads.

Through the screen she saw it was the older woman who'd been sitting in the rocker. She was holding a covered dish.

Trent looked at it and groaned. "Really, Violet?"

Shelby didn't know why he sounded grumpy. It smelled like cornbread and something else, maybe molasses. Whatever it was, the aroma was divine.

The woman glared at him. "You gonna let me in?" She was tiny, not even five feet, her voice surprisingly rough.

When Trent didn't respond, Shelby looked at him. Why the hesitancy? The woman was obviously his neighbor…

Unless…

Shelby hurried to open the door. "Of course, this is perfect timing," she said, then glanced at Trent, who sighed with disgust. She smiled sweetly. "You did say I could ask anyone."

# 2

ANYONE BUT VIOLET.

Damn, no telling what the old busybody would say. She'd stir the pot just to see what bubbled over. She did it to him all the time.

Shelby held the door open wide.

Trent didn't try to hide his irritation. "I see you're making yourself right at home."

"Thank you, dear," Violet said, smiling at Shelby as she crossed the threshold.

He didn't miss the shrewd gleam in the troublemaker's eye. Shaking his head, he caught the door when Shelby let it go and kept it open. "Violet, I know you're not one for visiting. Don't let us keep you."

"Don't mind him." Violet passed the foil-covered dish to Shelby. "Nobody does."

"As a matter of fact, this young lady isn't staying, either." He swatted at the fly he'd let in. "She needs to get to Blackfoot Falls before The Boarding House Inn is full."

Shelby shook her head and smiled at Violet. "I'm Shelby."

"Shelby, huh?" Violet completely ignored him. Which was what he generally preferred, just not at the moment. "What a pretty name. I'm Violet Merriweather."

"Nice to meet you, Ms. Merriweather." Shelby sniffed the dish she held. "Is this cornbread?"

"Homemade. Along with my own baked-beans recipe. It won me a blue ribbon at the 1989 county fair. I use a couple shots of bourbon. And, honey, I'd be pleased if you call me Violet."

Trent would call her a cab and gladly pay the fare all the way to California if he thought that would get rid of her. She hadn't been inside the house even once since he'd moved back. As far as he knew, anyway. Probably came in to snoop when he went to town for supplies.

"For pity's sake, Trent Kimball," Violet said, wildly waving a hand around. "Must you let in all these damn flies?"

"They were invited. You weren't."

When Shelby stared at him as if he had the manners of a baboon, he let the screen door slam. But only because the flies were getting out of hand. Good. Let Ms. I've-got-the-deed know what ranch life was like. Full of flies, hard work and no time for this kind of bullshit.

"I've been here eight months now, and this woman has never offered me so much as a crumb," he said, gesturing to Violet. "She's nosy and is up to no good. Plain and simple."

Shelby blinked. "I thought you said your family's been here for generations?"

Trent sighed. He needed a beer, or preferably a whole bottle of tequila.

"Ah. I see…" Violet said, her face lighting up as she gave Shelby a head-to-toe inspection. "You must be the wife."

"Wife?" Shelby darted him a stunned look. "His? God, no."

Trent clenched his jaw. He wasn't so much insulted by Shelby's reaction as he was pissed at Violet for bringing up his failed marriage. Which she was dying to know more about. She could be a pain in his ass but this was the first time she'd made it personal.

Signaling for Mutt to follow, Trent headed for the kitchen. It didn't matter that he glimpsed a trace of regret in the old woman's pale eyes. If remorse got her out of his house quicker, then good, otherwise he didn't give a shit.

After he'd filled Mutt's food bowl and the dog was wolfing down his supper, Trent grabbed a beer out of the fridge. The two women could stand out there yakking for the rest of the afternoon for all he cared. Let Violet do her worst. Hell, Shelby could bunk with her in the double-wide.

He twisted off the bottle cap, threw it at the trash can and missed. Maybe Violet's comment was innocent. She hadn't actually said anything about him being divorced. Not that he kept it a secret. He just didn't like talking about it. Especially when some things about Shelby reminded him of his ex. The way she dressed, for instance. Designer jeans and high-heel boots around here? And those soft slim hands, she couldn't use them for much. So what the hell did she want with a ranch, anyway?

A nagging thought finally took hold. Violet hadn't put him in a sour mood. Well, no more than normal. Shelby's horrified reaction at being mistaken for his wife had done it. Which made no sense. He didn't know the woman and only wanted to get rid of her. Sure, she was attractive but he honestly wasn't interested.

The horde of flies he'd let in weren't helping his mood. Jesus, they were everywhere. He swatted at the persistent little bastard buzzing near his ear. And missed. He had a mind to set out Violet's beans and cornbread. That should keep them busy for a while.

Dammit, that one fly seemed determined to drive Trent crazy. It dive-bombed his ear again. He stayed completely still for a few seconds, waiting, waiting for the perfect moment, then spun around and slapped…

Shelby. Right in the face.

He stared at her and she stared back, eyes wide, lips parted. He looked at his hand again. What the hell…

When he looked back at Shelby, she'd hardly moved. Or blinked. It was some kind of miracle that she hadn't dropped the casserole dish.

He went to take it from her and she reared back.

"Jesus, I didn't mean to… I was going for a fly…then you were…you were in the living room… I didn't hear you. I swear I would never…" He nodded at the dish that was starting to sag. "Maybe I should just take that from you?"

He moved slowly, wishing she'd stop staring at him like he was the devil himself. Thankfully, she let him have the dish with no fuss.

Her head tilted a smidge as she blinked. "You slapped me."

"No, I was— There was this fly," he said, wondering why, the one time in his life when he'd needed a fly, it had vanished into thin air. "I'm truly sorry. Let me see," he said, reaching for her.

She moved back again, lifting a tentative hand to her face.

"It wasn't on purpose." Trent couldn't see any kind of mark or discoloration but that didn't make him feel much better. He'd never hit a woman in his life, and he hoped to never do it again. Even by accident. "Why'd you sneak up on me?"

"I did no such thing."

"Sorry, I didn't mean… Please, let me have a look…"

"I'll live." She slowly flexed her jaw. "For your information I was bringing in the food, not sneaking up on you."

"What happened?" Violet rushed in with a concerned frown.

"I hit Shelby."

"It was an accident," she said, giving him an exasperated look.

"Well, I expect it had to be," Violet muttered. "Trent can be a stubborn jackass just like his great-grandpa, but he wouldn't strike a woman. Where did he get ya?"

"Really, it's nothing." Shelby turned her head, away from their prying eyes. "I could use something cold to drink."

He saw her eyeing his beer and he grabbed another one from the fridge. "What about you, Violet?"

"Wouldn't mind some whiskey if you got it."

No surprise there. He opened Shelby's beer and as he passed it to her, he snuck a look at her jaw. He doubted it would bruise, it hadn't been that hard. But that wasn't the point. Shit. He got out the Jack Daniel's from an upper cabinet, wondering if he could convince Shelby to use some ice on her face.

Violet took the bottle from him, then helped herself to a glass sitting on the draining rack.

He watched Shelby take an impressive gulp of beer. "How about—"

"No," she said, her voice firm. "Thank you."

"You don't even know what I was gonna say."

"No ice. I'm fine."

Trent hid a sigh by drinking his own beer. He hated when women did that. Pretended they could read your mind. He hated it even more when they were right. Well, screw that. "Not ice. I have a thick T-bone in the fridge."

Shelby let out a short laugh. "You're not serious."

He wasn't but she didn't need to know that.

"I'm not putting a slab of raw meat on my jaw."

"It's supposed to work for black eyes."

"That's a foolish, archaic old wives' tale."

"Good. Because I've changed my mind. I'm frying that steak for my supper."

Violet threw back a healthy shot of whiskey and poured another. "Is it big enough for all of us?"

"No." It wasn't enough that she was guzzling down his whiskey? She wanted his steak, too? He noticed Shelby checking out the silly daisy wallpaper he hadn't had time to get rid of yet.

"Yep," Violet muttered. "You're just like your great-grandpa. Cut from the same ornery mold."

Trent looked at her. "What was that crack earlier? I'm not stubborn, and neither was Gramps."

Violet snorted. "Like hell." She nodded at Shelby. "So was yours. I reckon that's why you two are here in this mess."

"Excuse me?" Shelby stared at her. "How could you know my grandfather?"

"Can't say I ever met *him*, but I knew your great-grand-daddy. You said your last name is Foster. Harold Foster was your great granddad, wasn't he?" Violet said, and Shelby nodded. "Harold was a kind, mild-mannered man most of the time."

"Wait. Hold on. What mess?" Trent asked, knowing in his gut he wouldn't like the answer. "Because I was doing just fine before…" He glanced at Shelby, saw her absently probing her jaw, felt a stab of guilt and closed his mouth.

"While you were in the kitchen swatting at flies, this young lady told me why she's here," Violet said, "and I've got a fair notion as to what might've happened."

Shelby's green eyes brightened. "You think I really do own the Eager Beaver?"

"Look here, Violet, you can't just make up stories because you're bored," Trent warned. "I swear to God, if you stir up trouble, I'm gonna sic Mutt on you."

Shelby inhaled sharply. "You wouldn't."

He ignored her, determined not to let Violet off the hook even if Mutt would just lick her to death. "This woman has driven all the way from Colorado and—"

"How do you know where I'm from? I didn't tell you."

"License plates."

"Oh."

He wished she'd quit wetting her lips and distracting him. "How's the jaw?"

"Don't change the subject."

"Well, excuse the hell out of me for being concerned." Trent started to take a pull of beer but pointed the bottle at Violet instead. "Tell her how long my family's owned this ranch. You ought to know. I remember you had that old brown trailer when I was a kid living here with my folks. You'd just gotten the double-wide when I visited Colby six years ago. Now, go on and tell Shelby that this property rightfully belongs to the Kimballs. Please."

Violet ignored him. As usual.

Shelby looked like all the air had left her lungs. If she hadn't been set on taking his last chance away from him, he would've felt sorry for her.

He turned back to Violet, who was watching the byplay as if she'd have to testify in court. "You have no intention of straightening this out, do you? Makes sense, since it would be the first nice thing you've done since I came back home. I don't even know why I let you stick around. I should've given you the boot."

Shelby gasped.

He looked at her. "What?"

"Could you be any ruder?"

"Sweetheart, you have no idea." Trent tossed back more beer, and then wiped the back of his hand across his mouth. "You got a problem with my etiquette, there's the door."

"Huh." Shelby sniffed with disdain. "I'm surprised you know such a big word."

"What?" He snorted. "You mean a Neanderthal like me?"

"Now you're just showing off."

Violet's rusty cackle reminded them she was still there. Shelby blushed and took a dainty sip.

He probably should've offered her a glass. "You gonna tell her, Violet? Instead of letting her get her hopes up." He did a quick once-over of Shelby, from the top of her tawny hair all the way down to her city boots. "Not that she'd last more than twenty minutes out here."

"Honey," she said, her chin lifting, "*you* have no idea."

Trent met her feisty green eyes. She had grit, he'd give her that, but with those dainty manicured hands and soft skin, she'd chosen the wrong zip code.

"Well, ain't you two a pair?" Violet muttered, sounding more troubled than amused. "It's like watching Harold and Edgar all over again. This isn't good. Not good at all."

They exchanged frowns, then both turned their attention to Violet.

Edgar was Trent's great-grandfather, though he'd died when Trent was eleven, so his memory of him might be a little fuzzy. "So, out with it," he said. "Say what you want to say."

"Pigheaded and impatient. You're just like him," she said, her fondness for Edgar obvious in the small smile tugging at her weathered mouth. She nodded at Shelby. "Harold was another one. You couldn't find a pair of mules more ornery than those two boys. Both of them twelve years my senior and acting like kids. Fighting all the time, mostly over nothing at all. Makes a body wonder how they ever became friends much less business partners."

He watched Violet pour more whiskey, then he glanced at Shelby. From the dread on her face, he figured she was thinking along the same lines as him. Hell, he sure hoped his folks had an honest-to-goodness deed in their possession or this could get sticky.

"Business partners," Shelby repeated. "What kind of business?"

"Well, the Eager Beaver, of course."

Trent muttered a quiet curse.

Sighing, Shelby rubbed her left temple.

Mutt stood at the kitchen door and barked. After Trent let him out, he saw Shelby frowning at the unsightly grooves on the doorframe, remnants from Mutt's habit of scratching to go outside. The job required the wood to be sanded before he could paint. It was on his to-do list along with a hundred other chores.

He had a feeling he was going to need another beer. The fridge door squeaked when he opened it. Just like the other dingy white appliances, the poor old Frigidaire was on its last leg. "Obviously the partnership didn't work out," he said, and nodded at Shelby's nearly empty bottle.

She shook her head. Her resigned expression should've made him feel better. It was clear Edgar had stayed and worked the ranch. Had Harold given up his share and moved to Colorado?

Violet wasn't looking smug as expected, but kind of glum, so he let her be and waited until she was ready to continue.

It was Shelby who finally broke the silence. "I'm not sure what any of this means. Are you saying my great-grandfather sold out to Edgar?"

Violet shrugged her narrow shoulders. "Can't say one way or the other."

Okay, Trent wasn't sticking around for any more of her tap dancing when the truth was plain as day. The tractor wasn't going to fix itself and he was losing daylight. It wouldn't kill him to let Shelby stay in the spare room for a night… Yeah, it could. Next thing he knew, she'd be moving her stuff in and taking over the house.

His gaze caught on the rise and fall of her breasts and

he had to remind himself he wasn't interested. Not in her, not in any woman. Now, he wasn't opposed to some recreational sex once in a while. But with Shelby? As his granddad used to say, Trent had as much chance as a one-legged man in a kicking contest.

"Some folks need to argue about everything. It's just their way. Those two even fought over naming the ranch," Violet continued. "Edgar claimed he saw a beaver over at Twin Creek reservoir, and Harold swore up and down it was a marmot. They finally flipped a coin."

"As fascinating as all this is," Trent said, grabbing the whiskey and returning it to the cabinet. "I have work to do."

Violet didn't protest being cut off, which was peculiar in itself. Then her faraway gaze drifted to the window over the sink, as if she'd slipped into her own little world. "Always arguing like those two did, no one ever paid them any mind…but that Saturday-night poker game at Len's they had a terrible falling out. Both of them with full-blown cases of booze blind, they said things they couldn't take back." She shook her head, the sadness in her face giving the room a chill. "Stupid old mules. A day later, Harold up and left."

He glanced at Shelby. Hugging herself, her expression sympathetic, she stared at Violet.

When Shelby turned to look at him, he avoided her eyes and took a swig of beer.

"What the hell did you do with my whiskey?" Violet had returned to the present with her usual cantankerous disposition, and Trent couldn't say he was sorry. At least it helped prove to Shelby that Violet was a nightmare.

"*Your* whiskey?" He put his empty beer bottle in the sink. "The tea party is over, ladies. I'm going back to work."

"Don't let us stop you." Violet pulled her pipe out of her pocket.

"On, no. Not in here, you don't. Put that away."

Violet huffed in annoyance.

Shelby cleared her throat. "So, I guess we're back to where we started."

Not from where he stood. Although she claimed to have a deed. And he didn't peg her for a liar. Obviously there was more to the story. "I'd be happy to give you directions to The Boarding House Inn. It's on Main Street. You can't miss it."

"Actually, I'll be staying here until one of us can prove ownership."

"Are you kidding me?"

"It's the only fair thing to do."

Violet chuckled. "Attagirl."

Mutt barked from outside the door.

"You can let him in on your way out," Trent said to Violet, who gave him the familiar glare, basically telling him to kiss her ass. He grinned. "Thanks for the beans and cornbread."

# 3

SHELBY WATCHED THE interplay between Trent and Violet. Any other time it might have amused her. Neither of them would admit it, but they liked being neighbors. They liked each other. Had it been that way with her great-grandfather and Edgar? Had their friendship been based on harmless banter and a genuine concern for each other…until it hadn't?

What had caused the final showdown, she wondered. Violet knew the answer, of that Shelby was quite certain. Just as she was convinced the older woman would never reveal it. Shelby didn't consider herself the romantic sort, but she couldn't help wondering if Violet had been the source of the trouble between the two men. Although she would've been fairly young.

Violet still had the pipe in her hand as she walked toward the door. "I reckon I'll go on home and leave you two to figure out sleeping arrangements."

Shelby and Trent looked at each other at the same time. Annoyingly, she felt a blush spread across her cheeks. She was quick to refocus her attention. Which happened to land on his left hand, his ring finger to be exact, and the pale mark that could easily be from a wedding band he'd once worn.

Violet had mistaken Shelby for his wife. Not ex-wife, and he hadn't corrected her so they were probably separated. Interesting that Violet didn't know the woman. Not that it made a difference to Shelby. He could have five wives for all she cared. Though she doubted he'd find that many women willing to put up with him.

He took her empty bottle and rinsed it out along with his. As he stood at the sink she got her first good look at his behind. His very nice behind. He was tall and muscular without being too husky, a body type she'd always appreciated. Okay, so he had a few decent assets.

A loud bark made her jump.

Just as the dog came bounding in, she caught Violet's mischievous grin. The woman had paused at the screen door and watched her ogle Trent.

Shelby did the only thing she could do. She smiled back. "Thank you for the food. I'll be sure to return your dish," she said. "Or maybe you'd like to join us for dinner?"

Trent turned, his eyes narrowed. "Excuse me, but this is still my house."

"Half," Shelby said. "Half your house. I think we can agree on that for the time being. Don't you?"

"Hell no."

Violet let out a howl of laughter as the screen slammed behind her. Shelby could see how her cackle might get on a person's nerves after a while. She bent to pet the dog's head and as the sound faded, watched Trent drop the rinsed bottles into a plastic milk crate, purposely ignoring her.

"I'll get my things from the car," she told him, not surprised when he didn't answer. "I hope there's a spare room."

"Nope."

"This is a three-bedroom house. You can't be sleeping in all three rooms."

"Yes, I could, but as it happens, I use one for storage." He paused. "And the third as my office."

She glanced at the laptop sitting on the table, then raised her brows at him. "I bet there's enough space for me to sleep."

"I have private stuff in there. I can't give just anyone access."

"Hmm, well, I suppose I'll have to take the couch."

"I watch TV late. Sometimes till three in the morning."

"No wonder you don't have time to keep the place up," she said, sweeping a gaze over the cracked linoleum floor and chipped Formica countertops, before returning to Trent.

His eyes had turned a steely gray. It made him look a bit dangerous, and she suppressed a shiver. "See, that's the beauty of owning my own place. I don't have to answer to anyone. And you know what else? The couch is mine."

She drew in a deep breath, refusing to look away. If she hadn't met the *other* Trent, the more affable man who'd teased Violet, the man who had seemed genuinely stricken over accidentally hitting her, Shelby would've left by now. She'd be too afraid to be in the house alone with him. Also, knowing Violet was next door helped.

No, she couldn't afford to lose ground now. What was that saying about possession accounting for nine-tenths of the law? "I'd like to see the storage room. And your office. Maybe we can move things around. I don't need much space." *For now.* Luckily, she'd noticed the perfect spot to make her jewelry.

He snorted a laugh. "Lady, you are something else. You wanna stick around, feel free to sleep in your car."

"I thought about it," she said, pleased that she'd surprised him. "But since neither of us can actually prove ownership, I don't think I should be inconvenienced."

Trent stared back, shaking his head. "You're willing to

stay in a house, alone, with a strange man. I could be a se-
rial killer, a bank robber, an ex-con—"

"With a whole town willing to vouch for you? I don't
think so." She smiled. "Shall I poke around on my own, or
do you want to show me the rest of the house?"

He folded his muscular arms across his chest. "Look
me in the eye and tell me you honestly don't believe this
dispute is going to turn out in my favor."

She blinked, once, then met his steady gaze. A jitter in
her tummy prevented her from speaking right away. This
last week had taught her several important lessons. Not the
least of which was to stop being a pushover, stop compro-
mising her individuality in order to be liked and to belong.

Shelby understood his anger. It appeared his ancestors
had stayed, hers had not. Trent was right. When the dust
settled, it was very likely she'd have no claim at all. But
in the meantime, in case there was the slimmest possibility she was entitled to even a fraction of the place, she'd
stay right here. Where she had the best chance of proving
she could stand on her own two feet. Enjoy the creative
freedom to design jewelry she loved without having her
work belittled.

"We have no way of knowing what happened to Harold and Edgar's partnership, or how it affected the ownership of the Eager Beaver," she said calmly, very aware
that she'd skirted the question.

Unless she was mistaken, Trent was seriously considering calling her on it. He studied her for a long excruciating
moment, then brushed past her without a word.

She followed him out of the kitchen and to the hall. She
took a quick peek down both sides. Only one bathroom.
That sucked.

"This is my bedroom," he said, motioning to his left, his
lips a thin straight line. "The one at the other end is yours."

The door was open. No furniture in her line of sight. Just ugly brown carpet. "Okay. What about—"

"We'll split the house in half. You stay on your side and I stay on mine. As soon as I get my hands on the deed, you're outta here. Agreed?"

"Well, no…" She poked her head into the no-frills bathroom. There was a shower-tub combo, a toilet, sink, no counter space to speak of, blue wallpaper from the eighties. But everything looked clean. "How are we supposed to divide the bathroom?"

"We're not. It's on my side. Feel free to use the john in the barn."

She turned back to him. "You're not serious."

"If the toilet gives you any trouble, shake the handle a few times. The shower is mostly used to get off the grime before coming in the house, so it's not enclosed. But don't worry. No one's gonna look."

Shelby stared into his smug face, while holding on to her temper by a thread. So this was how he wanted to play it. Clearly he'd forgotten a not so small detail. "All right, so I guess the kitchen is mine."

"Part of it."

"No, it's definitely on my side—"

He shouldered past her as if she were speaking to the wall.

"Where are you going?"

"Stay right there," he said as he put one booted foot in front of the other and paced off the room.

Diagonally.

"No," she said. "Stop. That's not how dividing works."

"You'll have the same square footage as me."

She tried to picture the kitchen. Exasperated, she couldn't remember it clearly, but she was pretty sure the sink, stove and fridge were not in her corner. Assuming she'd put up with this nonsense.

Yeah, when pigs fly.

"You're being a child," she told him.

He ignored her, disappeared into the kitchen, then reappeared holding up a roll of blue duct tape. "Just so you're clear on your areas."

"You're insane," she said, and caught a glimmer of a smile as he ran a long strip of tape across the hardwood floor. Of course that's what he wanted her to think so she'd get in her car and drive as far away as possible. "I'm surprised the tape can stick to all that dust."

He paused and gave the floor a thoughtful inspection. "To show you what a good guy I am, I'll loan you a broom so you can sweep your side." He frowned. "I almost forgot," he said and walked past her, back into the hall.

She found him standing just inside the door to her assigned room. Staring at a very nice unmade sleigh-style daybed that had been pushed against the beige wall. Blinds covered the lone window. "So, was this your storage room or your office?" she asked sweetly.

Trent's mouth curved in a slight smile. "Give me a few minutes and I'll get that out of your way."

The daybed? The mattress looked brand-new. And comfortable. She cursed her big mouth. "It's fine where it is. I wouldn't want to inconvenience you."

"No trouble."

Shelby watched him approach the bed. The brown carpet was looking less and less appealing. "Um, Trent…"

He cocked a brow.

Okay, humbling herself wouldn't kill her, but sleeping on the stained carpet might. "I would appreciate you leaving the bed." She cleared her throat. "Please."

Even as he made a show of mulling it over, humor glinted in his eyes. "You seem like a modern, independent woman. Just so you won't feel beholden, I'll rent it to you."

She sighed. "How much?"

"Hmm…let's see." Rubbing his jaw, he studied the bed. "Fifty bucks a night sound about right?"

"Fifty?" She paused to dial down her growing temper. Two could play this game. "Sounds high to me," she said, gingerly probing the spot where he'd clipped her. It didn't hurt in the least, but he didn't know that. "I guess I don't have much choice, though. I'm afraid the floor may be too hard."

Trent studied her, his expression that of a man who knew he'd been bested. "It's yours. On the house," he said walking past her. "Find your own sheets."

"Thank you," she called after him, and grinned when he cursed under his breath.

"YOU LIKE HER, don't you?" Trent shook his head at Mutt, who stood at the door whining to go after Shelby. "You're a damn traitor, that's what you are. Next time you want a treat, you'd better hope she packed some for you. She certainly has enough luggage," he muttered, watching her from the window as she pulled another suitcase out of her trunk, this one even bigger than the monstrosity she'd already carried to her room.

Mutt moved closer and barked at him.

"What? You just had your supper. And quit slobbering all over the linoleum. You want your new girlfriend to think you're uncouth?"

Trent wiped down the stained porcelain for the third time before he realized what he was doing. Hell, he didn't have to pretend to clean the kitchen sink just so he could keep an eye on her. Mutt didn't know the difference.

Anyway, this was still his house. His window. His damn driveway. He could look at anything he damned well pleased. He tossed the sponge aside, dried his hands and pushed his fingers through his hair.

The dog panted loudly, his long pink tongue hanging out of his mouth as he stared up at Trent.

"Forget it, buddy. I'm not going to help her. Why should I? She's lucky I don't call the sheriff and have her locked up for trespassing." In spite of himself, he looked outside again and watched her set a big cardboard box on the ground. "Hell, how deep is that trunk?"

Man, she had a lot of stuff. This was her third trip into the house. Each time she'd been loaded down with bags, pillows and whatnot. Hadn't she said her belongings were gonna be delivered next week? How much crap did she have? He shouldn't be surprised. Not after being married for three years.

She picked up the box, struggling to get a hold on it. She wasn't all that short, maybe five-six, but her arms couldn't make it all the way around. Stopping midway from her car to the walk, she set the box down. Or more like dropped it.

Mutt whimpered and ran back to the door, tail high and swishing back and forth.

"All right." Trent grabbed his hat off the peg behind the door and pointed at the dog. "You owe me."

By the time he made it to the porch, she was dragging the box up the front walk. She must've heard the screen's squeaky hinges because she looked up. "I assume I have a grace period to cross your side of the house until I finish unloading?"

Without a word he walked over, hefted the box and carried it to the porch, then left it there while he grabbed the suitcase. The suckers weighed a friggin' ton. Obviously she wasn't kidding about moving in.

"I didn't ask for your help," she said, a bit snippy when he crowded her off the stone walkway.

"You're welcome." He dropped the suitcase next to the box. "Anything else?"

"I'll get it." She started to turn and paused. "And thank you."

Trent watched her open the back door and lean across the seat. Gave him a real nice view of her butt. Naturally Violet was watching them from her porch. He wondered why she hadn't invited Shelby to stay with her. Just to fill her ears with a bunch of crap about him. Maybe create her own little reality show right here at the Eager Beaver.

He returned his attention to Shelby. Yep, a damn nice butt. Now if she knew how to cook, he might consider putting up with her for a week or so. Looked as though she planned to put down roots for longer than that. Damned if she didn't haul out another box the size of Wyoming. As with the other one, she could barely get her arms around the thing.

Sighing, Trent left the porch, taking the steps two at a time. "I've got it," he said.

The way she was bent over he could see right down her blouse. He forced himself to look away but not before he glimpsed the swell of her breasts plumping over a plain white bra. He didn't know why but he expected something snazzier. Red or black, maybe some lace. Though he was more interested in her...

"Did you hear me?" She straightened with a hand on her hip.

"Huh?" He met her accusing eyes. "Yeah, I heard you," he said and hoisted the heavy box.

"I said, I can manage."

"I'm not trying to be nice. You throw your back out and God knows when I'll ever get rid of you."

"Charming to a fault."

Sunlight shined directly on her face, and he was relieved there was no visible mark from his hand. She caught him staring and turned away to get another smaller bag from the backseat. The fact that striking her had been an accident wasn't making it any easier to ignore. She didn't seem to want to be fussed over. Earlier, though, in his old bedroom, when she'd touched her jaw, he had a feeling she might've been playing him. Didn't matter. Guilt nudged him either way.

Instead of leaving the box with the others, he set it just inside. He wasn't about to make the mistake of propping the door open and letting more flies in. By the time he moved everything off the porch, Shelby had joined him, carrying an overnight bag and a sack of groceries.

Puzzled, Trent grabbed the suitcase and smaller box, then led the way down the hall. This woman wasn't easy to peg. How she dressed, taking a chance on a place sight-unseen, out in the boonies no less. While she'd brought her own pillow, it seemed she'd been willing to sleep on the floor until her bed was delivered. Maybe she'd robbed a bank and was on the run.

He passed the room he actually was using for storage, and stopped at the one that had been his as a teenager. Holes from his old rodeo posters were still visible on the beige walls. The carpet didn't look too bad, though he imagined the dark color had a lot to do with that.

The wood blinds were slanted up to keep out the morning sun.

He'd completely forgotten about the pop-up trundle underneath the bare mattress, which fortunately, looked brand-new. If he remembered correctly the bed had occupied the second guest room back in Texas.

"If you don't like sleeping on a twin I can set up the trundle and push them together," he said.

"A twin is fine."

It took him a few seconds to remember he wasn't supposed to be making this easy on her. He set the suitcase near the closet and the box beside it. The contents clanged. Pots maybe? His gaze slid back to her sack of groceries.

"Is that it?"

Shelby frowned, puckering her lips in a way that made him forget what they were talking about. She turned to peek into the small closet and his eyes drew to her nice round backside.

He'd never understood why a woman would spend so much for designer jeans. He did now. Shelby turned to face him. Her eyebrows rose expectantly.

"Violet tell you this place is cursed?"

Shelby laughed. "No, she didn't."

"I'm not saying I believe it, but lots of folks do."

"Ah. I'll keep that in mind."

"I don't have to scare you off," he said, irritated by the amusement in her voice. "We both know you don't have a claim."

"If I thought that I would've left by now." She paused. "If you're so sure of yourself, why haven't you kicked me out?"

"Despite your low opinion of me, my mama raised me to be a gentleman." He couldn't say why her faint smile riled him. "If you've got any questions, I'll be outside."

"Aren't you worried I'll rob you blind?"

"Sorry, sweetheart—" Trent snorted a laugh "—someone else beat you to it."

$4$
___

THIRTY MINUTES LATER Shelby had hung some clothes and sorted her toiletries. The bathroom was small, typical of older homes, and sharing it with a virtual stranger wouldn't be easy. But it was better than having to trudge out to use the one in the barn. She really hoped he'd been teasing about that.

So she divided her makeup and personal hygiene stuff into two groups of must-have and optional, then packed them in smaller bags to take to the bathroom—wherever that turned out to be—with her as needed.

Fortunately she'd remembered to pack a couple of towels and her pillow but she'd forgotten about sheets. What was left of her jewelry-making supplies, though, those she'd kept close. It would've been so much easier to let the movers bring the boxes along with her furniture since it was doubtful she'd be setting up shop soon. She was low on just about everything she needed to make the silver and brass pieces that would bring in some good money. And she knew for sure she had to replace the old soldering iron. But after that awful scene with Donald, she'd been too hurt and angry to think straight.

She sighed, not eager to ask Trent for sheets. Maybe

she could lay a towel on the mattress and bring in the emergency blanket she kept in her trunk just in case she was ever stranded in foul weather. Along with it she kept a first-aid kit, a flashlight, batteries, bottles of water and power bars. Someone who was that careful should never have ended up in this mess. She wasn't normally impulsive; she was cautious, prepared for anything.

Except, of course, a broken engagement.

And a run-down ranch.

And no job.

Hopefully she wasn't starting a new trend, she thought, glancing around the small room. What the hell...there was a roof, walls; it was dusty but clean, and she hadn't had to pull out her credit card, so the situation wasn't completely awful.

Thinking back on the wedding gown she'd found just last week, she sighed. It had been love at first sight, and not because Mrs. Williamson would've disapproved of the retro style. Regardless of her ex-boss and erstwhile future mother-in-law's insistence, Shelby had never done anything to deliberately spite the woman. Shelby really did like trendy shoes and modern art, and a few other things Mrs. Williamson found vulgar. They simply had different tastes.

And Donald, well, he...

Shelby swallowed hard, trying to clear the lump in her throat.

Donald should've been on her side. Silly her, she'd misjudged his silence for support when she'd mentioned dusting off her old equipment and stretching her creative boundaries. But she could see the truth now. He'd assumed she'd be too busy designing pricy pieces for his parents' pretentious stores and inhabiting the role of Mrs. Donald Williamson to be bothered with her "tacky hobby." Well, screw him.

Sinking to the edge of the daybed, she traded her boots for well-worn sneakers and thought about making the dreaded call to her mom. Though not today. For one thing, it was the middle of the night in Germany where she was living with her new husband. But mostly, Shelby wasn't ready to listen to her mom go on and on about how Donald was a successful attorney, wealthy, handsome and a good provider. How Shelby would never have to work another day in her life. In one minute, Gloria Halstead could send feminism back a century.

Of course she'd call her father, too, but he had his hands full with his teenage stepchildren. He'd barely blink at the news. Just give her a verbal pat on the head and promise she'd find the *right one* soon. Which was completely fine with her. Shelby preferred his laidback approach to life. With her mom there was always so much drama.

She picked up her bag of groceries and wondered how serious Trent was over the whole dividing the house thing. Maybe he just needed to cool off. In the meantime, she could keep her perishables in the foam cooler she'd bought along the way. She went outside to fetch it from her car and saw Trent fiddling with something on the tractor. His T-shirt, damp with sweat, strained against his muscular frame. When he leaned across the engine, the worn denim of his jeans hugged his butt. Without his hat, his dark wavy hair gleamed in the late afternoon sun.

A tingle of awareness did something funny to her stomach. It wasn't difficult to ignore the unwanted reaction. Sure he was attractive, but annoying. And hadn't she just gotten rid of a pompous, annoying man?

Thinking of Donald again made her ache. Though not nearly enough considering they'd been dating for three whole years and engaged for ten months of that. This wasn't the first time she'd worried about not being more upset. Was it shock? When it wore off was she in for a heart-crushing plunge? After all, the wedding was planned for spring. They'd already decided on everything. She should feel devastated, not relieved. Or concerned over her faulty judgment in accepting his proposal.

Mutt spotted her first. He lifted his head from his shady nook in the grass, then came running toward her, tail wagging. Violet was nowhere in sight.

Trent's gaze followed the dog. His mood didn't seem to have improved. Whether because of the tractor or his comment about someone else robbing him blind, she didn't know. She figured he'd been referring to his wife, or ex-wife.

"Am I allowed to use the fridge?" she asked, shading her eyes to look at him. "I forgot."

"That's why I used tape. The stove, fridge and sink are all on my side." He eyed her sneakers, then her messy ponytail before turning back to the engine.

"Basically that means I have no access to water in the house."

"That would be correct."

God, she hoped he wasn't serious about the ridiculous setup. But then, what did she expect? She was a stranger, an intruder invading his space without warning… She bit her lip. See? Her judgment was completely messed up.

If it weren't for Violet living right on the property, Shelby would never have made the impulsive decision to stay. By the same token, it was Violet who had given her hope that Shelby's grandfather's bequest was valid. And if she ever needed a time for that to be true, it was now. She'd never felt so lost, not when her parents had divorced or when she'd changed high schools in the middle of junior year and immediately become the girl with the ugly glasses.

"Wait," he said, when she turned back toward the house. "I'm pissed off at this engine. I didn't mean to take it out on you."

"I don't blame you for being upset." She wasn't fibbing, though she'd also decided that being nice to him could benefit her restricted living conditions. "I appear out of the blue, disrupt your life. If the situation were reversed I'd be upset."

"Yeah, well…" He rubbed a hand down his face and rolled his neck, grimacing with the effort. "I've been doing some thinking. Obviously you didn't show up here on a whim. You believe you have a stake in the place, and from what Violet said, you just might," he said, squinting at her. Then yanked up the hem of his shirt and blotted the sweat from his eyes.

She stared at his bare belly, tanned and ridged with muscle. How did a cowboy get a six-pack like that?

"Don't get too excited."

With a soft gasp, she snapped her gaze up to his face. He hadn't caught her gawking. He was still wiping his face.

"Our great-grandpas might've been partners at some point, but it seems the Kimballs ended up sticking around and making something of the place."

Could've fooled her. The barn, even the sheds looked horribly run-down. With the exception of the large, freshly painted structure closest to the corral. "Is that the stable?"

"Yep."

"Do you have horses?"

"Why? You want those, too?"

Shelby bristled. Here she'd thought they were moving toward détente. Still, no point in antagonizing him. She forced a smile. "Just making conversation."

"I have two quarter horses. One is a racehorse. That's what I do—I train them."

"Oh." Now it made sense that the stable was in such great condition. Beside it was parked a very nice horse trailer that probably cost a chunk. "So you're not really a rancher or farmer."

"Nope."

"I thought I saw some chickens."

He studied her a moment. "I have a milk cow, too. But the horses are my main focus."

"May I see them?"

"I'm sure you will," he said, resigned. "Just not right now."

"Okay." She looked up at the sky, then toward the Rockies. "It's pretty around here." She smiled, and ignored the suspicion in his narrowed eyes. "Peaceful," she added, wondering if now was the time to ask again about using the fridge.

She had a better idea. "Well, sorry I bothered you. I came out to get something from my car." She popped open the trunk and lifted the cooler, then balanced it against her hip while she closed the trunk.

She slowly carried it down the walkway to the front door, fairly sure he was watching her. Halfway there he said, "Wait."

*Bingo.*

Him offering the fridge instead of her asking again would be better in the long run. Let him lord his generosity over her, she didn't care. She got her cocky grin in check before turning to him.

"While you're out here, I might as well show you to your bathroom," he said, nodding toward the barn, a little smile betraying his amusement.

She could only stare at him.

What a prick.

WHILE HE WAS still working outside, Shelby hurriedly took a shower. In the house. Afterward, she pulled on a pair of old khaki shorts and a comfy T-shirt, then wiped down everything, until the place was exactly as she'd found it, which was clean. Like the kitchen. It seemed he only had a thing against sweeping.

She hung her damp towel over the rod in her closet and considered her next move. The refrigerator was old and didn't have an icemaker. Something she'd discovered when she'd tried to swipe some fresh ice for the cooler. She hadn't dared touch the two trays. The jerk probably knew exactly how many cubes were in there. She supposed she could bargain with him, offer a trade of some sort. Maybe do the sweeping and mopping?

Trent had shown her the barn bathroom just as he'd promised. And she honestly couldn't tell if he meant to carry out his edict, threat, whatever it was. But the so-called bathroom was horrible. The toilet was semi-enclosed by two walls and stacked hay bales. And the shower was a joke. Anyone walking ten feet into the barn had a clear view of it. No way could he think she'd use the stupid thing. Probably wanted to see how long it would take before she begged.

He'd really had her going with all that talk about how it was possible she had a claim. Which made him showing her the outdoor pit of a bathroom seem cruel. It certainly set her on edge.

Once she'd calmed down and realized that was likely his game plan, she decided on her strategy. It wouldn't be light for much longer, but he was still cussing at the tractor when she walked to her car.

Mutt trotted over to her and Trent looked up. She opened her trunk, then glanced around, scoping out the floodlight under the eave of the barn, the pair on either side of the stable door.

"The bulb's burned out," Trent said, gesturing to the barn. "I'll get around to changing it sooner or later."

"No problem." She pulled the flashlight from her emergency kit, as well as extra batteries. Well, it was more of a spotlight, which was perfect, though she doubted she'd need it for long.

"I have a twelve-foot ladder if you want to change the bulb," he said and swung up into the tractor seat.

"Maybe I will." She smiled, closed the trunk. "But not today."

His eyes narrowed at her, but his curiosity was forgotten the second the engine started. "Yes!" He sunk back in his seat and stared up at the sky. "Thank you. Thank you. Thank you."

Shelby smiled. She couldn't have cared less about his tractor victory except that his improved mood might extend to her.

"Have you been working on it long?"

"A couple days." He gunned the engine, then turned to her. His gaze lingered on her bare legs, then swept to her T-shirt. The instant he met her eyes, the flicker of interest died, and his expression changed. "How about that, sweetheart? You might've brought me some luck."

The phony endearment grated on her ears. Letting it go was the smart thing to do. She suspected he'd meant to irritate her. Maybe not. Some guys were still Neanderthals. But for some reason she doubted Trent was one of them.

You can catch more flies with honey, she reminded herself. She forced a smile that she suspected came out all wrong. "Since it appears we'll be roommates for a while, I think we should be completely honest with each other."

"Come again?"

"Honest about—"

He angled toward her and ran a hand through his dark hair. "No, the first part."

Instead of fixating on the bunching bicep straining his sleeve she rolled her eyes. "Housemates, if you want to be technical, but not the point. You should know that I don't appreciate being called sweetheart."

His mouth curved in a lazy arrogant smile. "Good to know," he said and jumped down. "Now, you mind moving out of my way so I can finish up…sweetheart."

Shelby pressed her lips together. Why hadn't she seen that coming? No sense trying to reason with a mule. She told herself she'd be the bigger person and not respond in kind.

He motioned to her car. "Park closer to the stable." He picked up a toolbox and looked at her again. "By the way, we aren't roommates or housemates, whatever. Out of the goodness of my heart, you're my guest."

"You deprive all your guests of bathroom and kitchen privileges?"

"Only the unwanted ones," he said over his shoulder, already returning his attention to the tractor. "Which reminds me, later we'll go over your chores. Hope you're an early riser. Lots of work to be done on a ranch."

His back to her, she gave him a one-finger salute. And hoped Violet hadn't seen it from a window.

As Shelby rounded the front of her car, she noticed that he'd fixed the corral railings. Holding in a grin, she paused at the driver's door. "They're crooked."

"What?" He turned and frowned at her, before following her gaze.

"The rails." She tilted her head to the side. "They're slanting to the left."

"Like hell." He glanced back at her, then grudgingly mirrored her head angle to study his handiwork.

"I guess it doesn't matter." Afraid she couldn't keep a straight face, she opened the door. Yes, she was messing with him. The bastard deserved it.

"Which one?"

"Both," she said and slid into the leather bucket seat, grinning behind the tinted windows.

Trent smelled the beans and cornbread the second he entered the house. And something else that made his stomach growl. Ham, maybe? He didn't have any in the fridge or freezer. Shelby had to have brought it with her, or maybe the suddenly helpful Violet had made another delivery while he was watering the horses.

Earlier he'd made a tactical error. The microwave sat on a cart on Shelby's side of the kitchen. Had he thought quickly, he would've rolled it over to his side before he'd duct-taped the place. He used the microwave more than he did the stove or oven.

He ducked his head into the kitchen. Shelby wasn't there and no food had been left out. He checked the fridge and found only the beans and cornbread, so he took out leftover roasted chicken legs to go with it. Not that he had any idea how to heat up everything without the microwave.

He'd washed up some in the barn but he still needed a shower. The bathroom door was open, and the one to Shelby's room closed. Much as it irritated him, he returned to the kitchen and heaped a portion of the food onto a pie tin and stuck it in the oven at a low heat. He briefly considered cheating. All he had to do was keep the microwave from dinging, but if she caught him that would screw up everything.

They would have to renegotiate and he had no intention of making this easy on her. Not only was she trying to take his home away from him—the only home he had left—she was also killing him parading around in those shorts. She had great legs, and he figured she knew it. He'd finally managed to curb errant thoughts of sex during the day, and given himself free reign during showers and bedtime. In a matter of minutes she'd screwed that up for him.

Thinking about the expression on her face when she saw the barn bathroom made him feel better. Wouldn't have surprised him if she'd gotten in her car and left then and there. Damn, he wished she would have. It wasn't in his nature to be ugly like that, Violet notwithstanding.

But Shelby had recovered quickly. And he expected that she'd already snuck in a bathroom visit or two while he was outside. That didn't bother him. She'd be forced to go to the barn sooner or later, and just one time would do it. If the sorry condition of the toilet didn't, the feral cat that lived part-time in the barn would probably scare some sense into her. The woman didn't belong here. And Trent was just helping her see that.

The sooner she left, the happier he'd be. Working alone, his schedule was ruthless. Having to think about *her* was already costing him. So every time his inner voice said he'd never force a lady to use the barn bathroom, he shut it down. This was just another woman trying to take what was his. No warning. No nothing. He couldn't deal with another loss. Not now. Maybe never.

He took a faster shower than usual. Partly so his supper wouldn't burn, but mostly out of self-preservation. The moment his soapy hand had touched his cock, his thoughts had gone straight to Shelby. Instead of indulging, he'd turned the water on cold. And cursed her until all the soap ran off his body. It was a sorry day when a man couldn't even shower in peace.

Her bedroom door was still closed when he settled on the couch with his food and turned on the TV. He'd almost finished eating and was considering seconds when he heard her door open.

He knew she was moving around just behind him but he stayed focused on the television. If she was going outside she'd have to leave via the kitchen.

"Excuse me," she said. "Would you mind flipping on the porch light? It's on your side of the house."

"No problem." Holding back a grin, he rose with his plate in hand. "I put the stable lights on for—"

Shelby was naked.

Almost.

All she wore was a blue towel. It wrapped around her breasts, tucked in at the side and ended high on her thighs. Another towel was draped over her arm and she held a bar of soap in one hand, a flashlight in the other. On her feet she wore bright yellow flip-flops.

"It seems I forgot to pack my robe," she said, glancing down at herself. "I hope you don't mind. I'm just running out to the barn."

Trent couldn't find his voice. He couldn't look away. Trying to swallow didn't help. His mouth was too dry. "You were wrong," he finally muttered. "They weren't crooked." He flipped the light switch then walked past her, looking straight ahead, as if he had on blinders. "Go ahead, use the front door if you want."

"What wasn't crooked?"

Jesus, why had she followed him into the kitchen? "The rails." He set his plate and fork in the sink, and for the life of him, couldn't recall where he kept the dish detergent. "I used a level."

"Oh. False alarm. Sorry." She smelled good, standing somewhere behind him. Not that he was about to look. "Oops!"

He turned his head.

She was rearranging the towel. "Almost lost the sucker," she said, pulling the terrycloth snugger.

Her breasts swelled and plumped over the top with each small tug of the towel. He could barely drag his gaze away.

Talk about playing dirty. She was baiting him. And it

was working. All the blood and oxygen had rushed south leaving his brain to fend for itself.

Man, he didn't want to fold this early in the game.

He caught himself staring again and forced his attention back to the sink.

"Okay, well," she said, "thanks."

"Sure." He heard the kitchen door open and close, and he slowly lifted his head for a clear shot of her out the window.

Only he couldn't see her. What did she do, turn the wrong way? How could she miss the barn?

The hinges squeaked as the door opened. He barely had a second to lower his chin.

"I need to take some clothes. Or I'll have to come back in a wet towel," she said with a soft laugh as she crossed the kitchen.

It took all of a second for him to imagine her wearing nothing but a wet towel plastered to her body. His heart pounding like a Derby winner at the finish line, he ordered himself not to watch her exit, then gave up and looked. She was taking her sweet time, making a show of staying on her side of the duct tape.

The woman's legs were world class, no argument from him. And if he'd had the slightest doubt she was toying with him, it was gone. Guess it was time to prove he was made of stronger stuff than being a dope for a half-naked woman.

He turned to face her, leaned back against the counter and glanced at Mutt, who was curled up by the door. "Hey, boy." The dog looked up. Trent nodded at Shelby. "Fetch the towel."

She froze. Her eyes widened at Mutt, who had no clue what the command meant.

Trent smiled and watched her take off to her room as if she had the hounds of Baskerville on her heels.

# 5

SHELBY HEARD A noise and briefly opened one eye. It was still dark out so she buried her face in the pillow.

The pounding persisted.

She burrowed deeper, grabbing the scratchy blanket at her waist and pulling it over her head.

Someone was knocking, she realized, the exact moment the door opened.

"Shelby? It's five thirty. Rise and shine."

She peeled back the blanket and squinted at Trent, who'd poked his head in.

"You awake?" he asked.

"What?" She was still groggy. "Get out of my room."

"This is the second time I've knocked. Don't you go back to sleep."

The fog cleared. She felt around for something to throw and discovered her exposed butt. Tugging down the blanket, she scrambled into a sitting position. "Get out, or I swear I'll scream."

"That's okay. Everyone's already up," he said. "Come on. This is a ranch. We have hungry animals to feed."

Catching his smirk before he closed the door, she slid her head under the pillow. Who was he fooling? A ranch, her ass. Which reminded her… She knew she was wearing panties but wanted to be sure.

Groaning, she rolled off the bed and padded to the door. No lock. That's right. She'd checked last night. Dammit. She'd have to do something about that.

The sleepiness had worn off, thanks to her hospitable host, and she glanced around for her jeans and T-shirt. After grabbing the bag with her toothbrush and other toiletries, she stepped out of her room and stopped dead in front of the bathroom.

She muttered a curse, then headed for the kitchen, resenting the smell of coffee the whole way. How could she have forgotten to bring her single-cup brewer with her? She'd have to mooch some from Violet.

Trent was leaning against the counter with a steaming mug in his hand and a smug expression on his face. "You're welcome to a cup, this being your first day," he said as she continued to the door without a word. "Not a morning person, huh? You're living on a ranch now, sweetheart. Better get used to this."

She let the door slam behind her, not bothering to flip him off. If she gave in to every urge, she'd dislocate her finger. Too late she realized she should've brought her flashlight. It was that dark. And not a single light was on in Violet's trailer. Made Shelby wonder how much earlier than usual Trent had gotten up just to tick her off.

With only one cow, two horses and some chickens, how long did it take to feed the animals? She'd bet he normally didn't get out of bed until after seven. A pebble poked through her thin rubber flip-flops. She brought her foot up and hopped on the other the last yard to the barn.

She found the string to the bare bulb and a dim light showed her to the sink. It wasn't in very good shape. Until she'd wiped it down yesterday, the chipped bowl looked as if it hadn't been cleaned in years. And now mud was caked to the sides. Again. From Trent of course.

Today she was going into town. She didn't care how many chores he threw at her. She needed several jugs of water, a large bowl to use for things like brushing her teeth in her room, and maybe she'd pick up a set of sheets— she could always use spares, even after her stuff arrived. He thought if he made life difficult he'd send her running. The hell with him. She'd show him she was tougher than that. He wanted to show her rustic? Maybe she'd go really old school and keep a chamber pot in her bedroom.

Ew.

Nope. No way.

The thought alone creeped her out.

She saw something small and furry scurry across the hay-scattered ground and willed herself to ignore it. She got busy with her toothbrush and wondered what would happen if they discovered they each owned half, or even part, of the Eager Beaver.

She shuddered at the thought.

God, that name really had to go.

While she wasn't holding her breath about her chances, it was possible that she'd inherited part of the ranch. Which would send Trent through the roof. He'd do everything he could to make her life miserable.

So much for the quiet peaceful place she'd envisioned.

Last night, traipsing around in the towel, she'd thought she had him for a few minutes. Subtle, he was not. He'd been ogling her since she'd stepped out of the car.

If she was honest, and she needed to be, she'd done some ogling herself. But that wasn't the point. For the first time in her life, she'd used her sexuality to try and get her way. She'd lost. Okay, fine. But doing that wasn't *her*. She felt nothing but shame for stooping so low.

They needed to have a talk. Admittedly, the situation

was sudden and awkward. But now that he'd had some time to get used to her, maybe he'd be willing to listen and have a serious, adult discussion. And rip off the silly tape and give her full access to the house.

While rinsing out her mouth she thought she heard something. She turned off the water, quit swishing and listened.

Clucking.

There were chickens. A whole flock. Right behind her. Near her feet. Everywhere. Pecking at the ground between frenzied squawking and wing flapping.

Shelby shrieked when one pecked her bare toe. It didn't hurt. Just scared the crap out of her.

"Hungry this morning, aren't you?" Trent pretended to ignore her, smiling at the chickens as he scattered feed on the ground around her. "I know it's late. But don't blame Shelby."

So much for having an adult discussion.

"You're pathetic," she said, stepping over the noisy hens, and trying to get away. "No wonder you're divorced."

His head came up. Their eyes met.

He looked stunned. As stunned as Shelby herself felt. She didn't know if he was divorced, but she never should have said that. It wasn't like her to be so mean.

"Hell, you're probably right." He shrugged, as if her words hadn't fazed him, and threw a final handful of feed. But he couldn't hide the hurt in his expression.

She watched him walk out of the barn, shame taking a bite out of her. Just because he was being an ass didn't mean she had to be one. Unless he cut off her access to coffee. Then all bets were off.

BY MIDMORNING TRENT had finished his barn chores and was almost done with the tractor when he heard the kitchen door slam. He watched Shelby walk to her car and get behind the wheel. She hadn't mentioned where she was off to, and he wasn't about to ask.

He wasn't sorry he woke her up so god-awful early. A lot earlier than he'd risen since he'd moved here. Getting her up at dawn was only right. Thanks to her, he'd tossed and turned most of the night. Jacking off normally relaxed him. But he hadn't been able to do it without thinking of all that silky skin of hers. Or how her habit of nibbling at her lower lip made her look sweet and vulnerable. He couldn't afford to think of her in that light. Or he'd feel as if he was throwing her out, putting her on the street. It wasn't his fault that she'd have to find some other accommodations.

He didn't know what she did for a living but whatever it was she obviously was doing okay. She could afford that nice car. As for him, this ranch meant everything. He'd put a lot of money and sweat into building the stable and making the place suitable for training. For all the bellyaching he'd done about trying to whip the Eager Beaver back into shape, he was proud of what he'd accomplished. He wasn't about to let his hard work and dreams go down the drain.

He had a good shot at restoring his reputation and returning to doing what he loved best. Even winning some serious money in the bargain. Solomon had already won two races, and placed in a third. If the gelding could win just a few more decent purses, Trent would not only have enough wins to remind owners he was still in the game, he'd also have the resources for more improvements to the ranch. Might even be able to hire some help so he could concentrate solely on training.

He watched her taillights disappear from view, then turned back to the tractor. All he had to do now was change the oil and he was in business. The engine might've taken a while but he was becoming a better mechanic as well as a decent carpenter.

"Why the hell'd you feed my chickens?" Violet seldom left her porch, but she came up right behind him.

Trent sighed, wondering what he'd done to deserve Violet.

"The noise wasn't bad enough to wake everyone for a mile but you had to use half my scratch, too? That should've lasted them four more days."

He knew she had some in reserve because he'd fixed her feed bin the last time she'd left to do her monthly shopping. "I'll pick up an extra sack next time I go to town."

She squinted up at him from under the same brown battered hat she'd owned since he was a kid. "You never feed them. Must've had something to do with tormenting that poor girl."

"Poor girl? I sure didn't hear you offering her a place to sleep. I know you got a second bedroom in that trailer."

"Don't be a jackass." She turned toward the road but even the dust had already settled. "Is she coming back or did she leave for good?"

"Her clothes are still here." He only knew because she hadn't taken the suitcase with her.

"You find out what made her show up out of the blue like that?"

"No." Trent hesitated. "You?"

She shook her head. "Haven't talked to her at all today."

"Come on, Violet, give it to me straight. Do you think she has a claim?"

"Hard to say."

He didn't like the sound of that. There was no mischief in the woman's face or voice, so he had to believe this mix-up wasn't as cut and dried as he'd expected it to be.

"Have you talked to your pa yet?"

He shook his head. "They're visiting my sister and her family in Wyoming," he said, and rubbed at his tired eyes.

"I should call though. Even if they can't get their hands on the paperwork they might know something."

Violet was staring at him, her leathery skin wrinkling around her pinched mouth. "You look like crap."

"Thanks."

"You get any sleep?"

"Not much."

She chuckled. "Nope, I don't imagine you did."

He took off his hat and slapped it against his thigh, sending up a cloud of dust just as Violet pulled her pipe out of her pocket. She glared at him.

Trent laughed. "I didn't do it on purpose. Are you ever gonna cut me some slack?" he asked, and caught the beginning of a small smile as she turned toward her double-wide.

"I got a pot of stew simmering. Should be ready in an hour if you're hungry."

Okay, now she was scaring him. He watched her climb the steps and disappear into the trailer without giving him another glance. Violet being nice to him had to mean something was about to blow up in his face.

Since he never kept his cell on him while he was working, he went inside and found it in the charger. His parents disliked cell phones, only used a prepaid one in case of an emergency when they traveled. So he called his sister's landline.

His mother answered.

"Hey, Mom."

"Trent? Is anything wrong?"

"No. Everything's fine." Yeah, he knew he didn't call them often enough. "How are you and Dad?"

"We're good. Happy to see the grandkids. I swear your nephew has grown a foot since Christmas."

"I bet. Emily and Ron are all right?"

"Yes." She paused. "Trent Edgar Kimball, you better not be lying to me. Something is wrong. I can feel it."

"No, Mom, nothing. I promise." It bothered him to picture her face, flushed with worry. Course she fretted about everything while letting his father make the big decisions. Which hadn't always worked out so well for them. "I have a question about the Eager Beaver, that's all. I was wondering if you had the deed in your safe deposit box at the bank."

"Well, huh. I'm not sure. Hold on. Let me ask your dad." There was talking and laughter in the background, then her muffled voice, "Bob, it's Trent. He wants to know if we have the deed to the Eager Beaver."

The long silence that followed made him edgy. He walked to the window and peered between the blinds. Not that he expected Shelby home this soon. She'd probably just arrived in town. Assuming that's where she was headed.

"Trent?"

"I'm here, Mom."

"Your father doesn't remember what kind of paperwork we have. He's assuming it's a deed since there was never a mortgage on the place. Your grandfather paid off any debts long before he passed it down to your dad. I know for certain we have nothing on the lease agreement with Violet. That was a handshake deal. Why are you asking?"

"What lease agreement?"

"Oh, honey, I'm not sure. It's from years ago. Hold on. Your father is talking to me at the same time. What is it, Bob?"

Trent heard his dad's voice but nothing he could make out. It would be simpler if he got on the phone and explained himself, but he wouldn't. He liked to pretend he had a head for business, which couldn't be further from the truth. So he always seemed to find a middleman he could blame for any "miscommunications." Trent loved his dad but he'd never wanted to follow in his footsteps.

Whatever the man's faults, though, his parents seemed to have a happy marriage and that was good enough in Trent's book. Hell, he'd failed at keeping his own marriage intact.

"Trent? Your dad says the deal was between Violet and your great-grandfather. She can stay on the land as long as she wants in exchange for paying the taxes. As far as checking on the deed, I can go to the bank next Wednesday. We should be home the night before."

"Nobody told me about Violet," he muttered, thinking about all those times she'd pissed him off and he'd threatened to give her the boot. She'd never said a word about her lease deal. Course she knew he wasn't serious. They just liked to rile each other. But still…

"She's been there forever. No one really thought anything of it. Why are you asking about the deed?" She let out a soft gasp then lowered her voice. "You're not in financial trouble, are you, honey?"

"No, Mom. Nothing like that. Does the name Harold Foster ring a bell? Don't ask Dad," he added quickly. The last thing he needed was everyone making a big issue out of this. Or his dad blowing smoke. "I'm just curious."

"Foster. Sounds familiar. Sure you don't want me to ask?"

"Actually, I'd prefer you don't bring it up at all."

"All right." She knew not to ask why. Sometimes the Eager Beaver could be a touchy issue between Trent and his dad, who liked to go on and on about the curse. "I'll call you next Wednesday after I go to the bank."

"Thanks. Say hey to everyone for me."

"I will. Can I tell them we'll see you for Thanksgiving?"

"Wouldn't miss it." He hung up, still confused, and a little angry.

The deal with Violet… He could see how it was one of those things everyone just accepted and never spoke of. Especially since the ranch had been abandoned twice, each

time for a few years. It was probably a good thing Violet
had been around to deter vandalism or squatting. What
bothered him was the feeling he had that Violet knew more
than she was letting on. Even after denying it to his face
less than an hour ago.

THE PEOPLE IN Blackfoot Falls seemed friendly. And, naturally, curious. But not nearly as curious as Shelby had
expected. She hoped that meant a lot of tourists passed
through. If so, that would be excellent for her. She might
be able to find a shop owner willing to sell her jewelry on
consignment. Though she was getting a bit ahead of herself. So far all she'd done was cruise down Main Street to
get her bearings, then parked and walked two blocks to
Abe's Variety Store.

Not too many folks were out. She'd noticed the parking lot at the Food Mart was crowded, probably because it
was Saturday. Though she suspected weekends in a ranching community meant something different than they did
for city people.

Most everyone smiled or nodded to her. A couple of
young women stared, but that was it. Folks must've pegged
her for a tourist or visiting relative. The town was small
enough that a stranger would stick out.

She stopped outside the variety store and scanned the
bulletin board. There was a flyer for the county fair, another announcing Halloween happenings for the kiddies.
Also, ads for sale items, but no upcoming festivals. That
was a bummer. Her jewelry would sell well at a festival.
Although she hadn't actually tried to sell any of her pieces
since college.

After she'd started working as a designer for the Williamsons, she'd given the items she made on the side as
gifts. God forbid her *tacky* private pieces be associated
with the snooty Williamson Jewelers in any way. No, they'd

practically owned her. Too bad it had taken her so long to see that.

A bell above the door jingled as she stepped inside the store. The older man behind the counter looked up. One of the women he was talking to turned and gave her the once-over. Shelby just smiled and went in search of sheets. Although, judging by the size of the store and the type of merchandise she could see on the front shelves, she wasn't expecting much.

"Anything I can help you with, young lady?" The man from behind the counter approached just as she found a package of sheets.

"Hi. I don't suppose you have any colors besides white?" Or with a decent thread count, she thought, but kept that to herself.

"Not in stock, no. But I can order any color and size you want." He frowned at her over the glasses resting on his bulbous nose. "I figured you were staying at the Sundance, but then you wouldn't be needing sheets."

"The Sundance?"

"It's part dude ranch. Owned by the McAllister family," he said, waiting expectantly for her to fill in the blanks.

"I'm staying at the Eager Beaver."

"Okay." He nodded. "The Kimballs' place. You must be a friend of Trent's."

Her heart sank. "Um, not exactly," she said and realized too late she should've gone with his assumption.

"You can't be related to Violet. I don't believe she has any family."

*The Kimballs' place* kept echoing in her brain. "By the way, I'm Shelby," she said and gave him a bright smile.

"I'm Abe, like it says out front." He scratched his balding head.

"Have you lived here long, Abe?" She kept her tone casual and picked up a plastic-wrapped pillowcase.

"All my life."

"Then you must know the Kimballs pretty well."

"Oh, yeah, I went to school with Trent's pa. Bob and I used to go hunting together. Now, how is it you're related to the family?"

"Actually, my last name is Foster." She looked for a sign of recognition in his face and found none. "My great-grandfather and Trent's were partners at the Eager Beaver."

He reared back with a look of surprise. "When was that?"

"Well, way, way before your time, of course."

Her subtle compliment registered, and she caught his blush before he turned away. "Louise, Sadie, come over here a minute, would ya?"

It took all of three seconds for the two women to sidle up to him and check her out.

"This here is Sadie." He gestured to the fifty-something brunette with a warm smile. "She owns the Watering Hole."

"And I'm also running for mayor." She stuck her hand out. "And you are?"

"Good grief, woman, do you always have to jump the gun?" Abe gave a snort of disgust, sounding much like Trent with Violet.

"Shelby." She grinned and shook Sadie's hand.

"I'm Louise," the other woman chimed in. "Part owner of the fabric store down the block. So, you're staying out at the Kimballs' ranch."

Shelby held in a sigh. Yes, it was clear the women were eavesdropping, but it was the *Kimballs' ranch* reference that got to her. Again.

"Do you two even wanna know why I asked you over here?" Abe looked from one to the other.

"Foster doesn't ring a bell with me, either," Louise said.

Sadie was frowning and shaking her head.

Abe threw up his hands and walked away.

For the next two hours, Shelby explored the town and heard "oh, the Kimballs' ranch" so many times she wanted to scream.

Sadly, she was starting to like the name Eager Beaver.

# 6

TRENT WAS IN the stable when he heard the car pull up. Shelby had been gone most of the day, and he'd wondered if she'd driven all the way to Kalispell. He waited until the car door opened and closed before he strolled outside.

She grabbed an armful of packages from the backseat and immediately dropped one. He didn't make it to her in time to pick it up. She scooped it up herself. Standing back, he watched her redistribute her haul and close the door with her hip.

"Need help?"

"No, thank you." She gave him a small polite smile, then started toward the kitchen door.

If she was still pissed at him over the stunt he'd pulled this morning, he couldn't tell. She didn't seem to be in a particularly bad mood but more resigned. Asking around town about the Eager Beaver had probably dashed her hopes.

Feeling like he was on shaky ground himself, he understood completely. After hanging up with his mom, he'd called Colby. His brother hadn't heard anything about Foster, or the deal with Violet, either. But that didn't make Trent feel any less like a damn fool, and he'd wasted half the day because of it.

And here he had so much to do. Yet he'd been working in fits and starts, preoccupied with memories of the times he and Violet had bickered over one thing or another. A couple of those instances had ended with him threatening to kick her off the ranch. Anyway, she always gave as good as she got. But how smug she must've felt inside. To give her credit, she'd never shown it. He had a feeling she knew he had a soft spot for her, but that was a fact he would never, ever acknowledge.

So far, he hadn't said a word to her about the conversation with his mom. He wasn't sure why since she might be able to put his fears to rest. His fear that Shelby had a legitimate claim. That he would have to buy her out or divvy up the place with her. Yeah, he still had some money, but he wanted it to go toward horses and training expenses. He couldn't afford to start over again.

The more he thought about the situation, the weirder it seemed. Violet loved a good argument and she liked poking at him but she'd never been outright mean. If she knew something that would settle the dispute with Shelby, he figured she'd speak up.

Maybe she was keeping quiet to protect him.

The thought made his stomach turn.

He glanced at the double-wide. Violet, who sat on her porch every afternoon, rain or shine, was nowhere to be seen. Beyond the trailer clouds were gathering over the foothills. In another hour or so it would be dark. He decided to finish cleaning his saddle tomorrow and tossed aside the rag and went inside.

Shelby's door was closed and he could hear her moving around in her room. After finding out how deep the Kimball roots went, maybe she was packing. The thought cheered him. He held nothing against the woman, but the sooner he got her and her tempting backside out of here the better.

He'd skipped lunch and still wasn't hungry. But with his improved mood he figured he'd heat the leftover beans and cornbread, maybe broil the T-bone after he took a shower. The steak was big enough to share with Shelby. After all, he wouldn't want to send her off hungry.

Thirty minutes later he'd finished showering and was checking the food in the oven when Shelby entered the kitchen. She was wearing old faded jeans and a snug white T-shirt that came to just above her waist and exposed a narrow strip of skin. They didn't seem like traveling clothes.

Not that he was capable of being all that logical. It wasn't only the unexpected peek that had his heart accelerating. Wearing this getup she was giving him a real good look at her shape. Small waist, nice curvy hips, not too thin. To his mind, the perfect woman's body. What he couldn't figure out was how his mouth could water and go dry at the same time.

"Be careful," she said, just as his thumb made contact with the blistering hot casserole dish.

"Son of a—" He jerked his hand away and burned the back of his knuckle on the oven rack.

Trent managed to bite off a pithy four-letter word. His damn thumb felt like it was on fire.

Slowly shaking her head, Shelby stared at his hand. "Ever heard of an oven mitt?"

"Your concern is touching."

"I'd have a look," she said, glancing at the blue tape on the linoleum. "But you're too far over. I'd have to cross into enemy territory."

"Very funny." He couldn't remember if he was supposed to use cold water or not. "For your information, I was heating this up for the two of us. And I was even gonna throw in the T-bone."

Shelby's gaze slid to the steak on the counter. "You're going to let a minor burn stop you?"

Sighing, Trent used the toe of his boot to kick the oven door shut. His thumb was pretty red, so were his knuckles. It wouldn't be fun wearing work gloves tomorrow.

"Seriously, you should run cold water over that hand then apply some Neosporin. If you don't have any, I've got a first-aid kit in my car."

"Worried you won't get dinner?"

"I am," she said with a smile, but he could see that she was genuinely concerned.

Maybe he needed to take it more seriously. While she frowned at his thumb, he studied her face. She had a cute nose. A weird thing for him to notice. Crazy long lashes. Could be fake but he didn't think so since she wore minimal makeup.

She did that thing with her bottom lip again. "You might want to wrap some gauze around it overnight."

"You some kind of burn expert?"

Holding her hand up, she showed him a mean scar on her inner wrist. "I have a couple more. Which you won't see."

That sent his mind scrambling to dark erotic places. "Arsonist?"

Shelby grinned. "I make jewelry. Sometimes I use a torch."

Trent turned on the faucet and let the cold water ease the sting. "A torch, huh? What kind of jewelry?"

"Do you still want the oven on?"

He figured he'd stay away from the broiler and fry the steak. "Off, please," he said, finally noticing the small bag in her hand. Last night she'd carried it out to the barn with her.

Neither of them mentioned her crossing the tape to get to the oven. He had to admit, the whole dividing-the-house-in-half thing seemed silly now. Not that he'd give voice to the admission. If he pulled the tape up, he wondered if the issue could die a natural death?

"Should I take the food out?" she asked.

"Mind checking it first? I forget if I got that far."

She grabbed the dishtowel hanging from a cabinet door and used it as a potholder. "I think it'll be fine left in the oven. You'll be eating soon, right?"

"About ten minutes. Will you be ready?"

She closed the oven door and straightened. Then glanced at the large round wall clock, taking a long time to make up her mind. "Sure."

He turned off the water and she tossed him the dish-towel.

"Ten minutes," she confirmed and headed for the door.

"Where are you going?"

Pushing the screen open, she gave him a wry smile. She started to step outside when an eerie howl pierced the air.

Shelby froze. "What was that?"

"A coyote. Didn't I warn you about them?" His thumb began to throb. Probably punishing him for teasing her. "They mostly stay in the foothills and on the ridges."

"Mostly?"

More frantic howling and yapping exploded. The noise he'd long grown accustomed to and unconsciously dis-missed had her taking a step back. She jerked her hands away and let the screen slam.

"I know it sounds bad," he said. "Some people think it's a feeding frenzy. But it's just the pack communicat-ing with each other."

"Saying what? Dinner's about to walk out the kitchen door?"

Trent grinned. "They're not even close by. Coyotes stay away from people. I promise, they're more afraid of you than you are of them."

"I doubt that." She moved forward a few inches. "Re-member, a lot of people in town know I'm staying here.

You don't want to have to explain my sudden disappearance."

"Hell, that's nothing. All I'd have to say is you tucked tail and ran back to the city. They'd get it." He laughed at her eye-roll and reached for the heavy wood door to shut out the noise.

"Wait." She put a hand on his arm, then drew back. "I need to go to the barn."

He sighed. "No, you don't."

"Are you kidding? I've had to go for five minutes."

"No, I meant…" He shook his head. They were close. Too close. Her scent did something unsettling to him. "No more boundaries. Use any room you want," he said, reaching again for the door.

"No. You said they won't hurt me." She cleared her throat. "I'm fine," she said, despite the fact that she'd gone pale. "The barn is fine." She lifted her chin and pushed the screen open.

"Come on, Shelby." He caught her wrist and tugged her around to face him. "Are you going to make me say it?" She blinked, then stared into his eyes. "Fine," he said. "Dividing the house, all this duct tape, I was being a dumb ass, okay? I've admitted it."

Another loud howl.

She jumped.

He drew her closer. Just so he could shut the door, he told himself. Not because she smelled so damn good it was driving him crazy. Or because her bright green eyes hit him square in the gut.

"I'm not going to go running back to Denver," she whispered. "Sorry, but I'm not." She let out a shaky breath. "I can't."

"Okay." He brushed the hair away from her cheek, reluctant to lower his hand. Damn, she was soft. "I was only teasing."

"No, you weren't," she murmured, a tiny smile twitching at the corners of her lush lips.

He shrugged a shoulder. "Half and half."

Her gaze flickered to his mouth. "I understand your position. I do. If I were you, I'd probably be furious."

"Probably?"

With a short exasperated sigh, she met his eyes. "An attorney contacted me. Explained that I'd inherited the Eager Beaver. I didn't get too excited at first but—I mean, what would you have done?"

"I know I wouldn't have packed up and moved everything before I even saw the place."

Her shoulders sagged. "This is so unlike me. It's insane, right?" She sidestepped him.

And boy did he want to kick himself. He hadn't meant to chase her off, though it was for the best. No use him getting soft now. Like wondering if she'd left Denver because she'd lost her job or suffered a nasty divorce.

He turned and watched her leave the kitchen. "What about dinner?"

"Bathroom first," she called back.

"Got it." He looked at his thumb. The sucker was red and throbbing.

After getting out the frying pan and setting it on the stove to heat, he went to get a cube of ice. The list of chores he'd stuck to the fridge was still there. He wondered if Shelby had seen it. He yanked the paper down and dropped it in the wastebasket under the sink.

She wasn't off the hook. Plenty of work around the place and she'd have to do her share. Though not necessarily the unpleasant things he'd initially had planned for her. Like milk Daisy. That cow had to be the moodiest animal he'd ever run across. More trouble than she was worth. He didn't even like milk all that much. Violet used most of it. He knew it made more sense to get rid of Daisy, but he didn't want to see her butchered. Not that he'd ever admit it. Especially not around here in cattle country. He'd get shit from Blackfoot Falls to Twin Creeks.

The ice was beginning to help. With his good hand, he unwrapped and seasoned the steak, then carefully set the T-bone in the frying pan. He didn't need another burn. At least the knuckles weren't so bad.

Behind him, Shelby noisily cleared her throat. She was holding up a tube of Neosporin. "I brought some gauze, too. I can wrap your thumb for you." She shrugged. "If you want…"

She hadn't changed her clothes, hadn't even brushed her hair, and yet she looked even better than a few minutes ago. No explaining why. Her shy smile faded. She lowered the tube.

"Yes," he said, stepping forward. "I'd appreciate it."

Shelby waited for him to extend his hand, then she inspected the burns. "I don't think your knuckles need wrapping," she said, after applying the antibiotic. "But your thumb, definitely. Does it sting?"

"Um…not too bad," he lied and saw she was trying not to smile. He tried to hold back a wince while she gently spread the white ointment.

To distract himself, he focused on her necklace. Jewelry wasn't something he usually noticed. But the purple pendant hanging from a silver chain was interesting. Gold flecks and veins caught the light and seemed to shift with her movement. "Did you make that?"

"What?" She looked up and touched the necklace. "Ah, yes. A long time ago."

"Nice."

With a brief smile, she unrolled a piece of gauze. For some reason, it seemed as if she didn't believe him.

"That's not a stone, is it?"

She shook her head.

"So, that's the sort of style you make?"

"Not since college." Her obvious reluctance to talk about her work baffled him.

"You might make great jewelry but your salesmanship needs work."

Shelby looked up again and laughed. "I'm not trying to sell you anything."

"You should be. My sister would go nuts over something like that. If I get her another scarf and wallet for Christmas, she'll disown me."

"Gee, I can't imagine why." She paid close attention while she wrapped the gauze then used a small pair of scissors to snip the excess.

"I'm serious. You're really talented."

She finished off the dressing with tape. "There you go," she said, purposely ignoring his comment. "Maybe between this and the ice your thumb won't swell and you'll heal quickly."

"Thanks," Trent murmured, appreciative but irritated. "What, you think I'm a country bumpkin with no taste?"

Her green eyes widened. "Of course not. It's just— Well, this isn't exactly fine jewelry."

"Nope. It's not. Believe me, I've bought my share of the expensive crap. Just ask my ex-wife." Trent hadn't meant to throw in the sarcastic remark, and he quickly moved on. "This is different, and it's really nice. Better than nice."

Shelby blinked and glanced down at the pendant. "Thank you," she said in a small quiet voice. "That means a lot."

Weirdly, he believed she was being truthful. His praise had meant something to her. And that gave him the uncomfortable feeling someone had done a number on Shelby's confidence. Even more weird, it pissed him off.

*Keep your distance, Kimball. She isn't your friend.*

"I plan on going back to working with turquoise and

silver and maybe fire art like this while I'm here." Excitement had crept into her voice. "Hopefully I haven't lost my touch."

"Good. I need to score points with my sister. I give Emily something like that for Christmas, she'll keep me in chocolate-chip cookies for a year."

Shelby laughed.

He gestured to the pendant. "You mind?"

For a second she looked startled. "Sure," she said, lifting it off her shirt. "Or I can take it off."

"No need. I just want a quickie."

She coughed, or laughed. Maybe both.

Trent sighed. "I meant a quick look—"

"It's okay. I know."

The chain put the pendant at collarbone level. He carefully took it from her and angled it to the left, then right.

"How did you do this?" he asked, more impressed each time the light caught on another deep rich color.

"Trade secret."

He glanced up.

She was smiling. "I'll show you some time. It's pretty cool."

Trent couldn't drag his gaze away from her perfect pink lips, how they parted slightly. How she might be thinking along the same lines as him. But even one kiss could be trouble.

Shelby took a deep breath that made her chest rise. He released the pendant, but she stayed right where she was. Close. Close enough that all he had to do was lean in a few inches…

She didn't move. Stayed completely still when he brushed his lips across hers. And then she lifted herself on tiptoes a little, just enough to increase the pressure of the light kiss.

Taking his cue, Trent pressed his mouth more firmly against hers. Her lips were soft and yielding, her breath warm and sweet, slipping out in a tiny, tempting puff. She surprised him by putting a tentative hand on his chest and leaning slightly into him. Her shy initiative was enough to take a nip out of his self-control.

Tongues became involved, and he put a hand on her waist. His fingers met with the silky skin below the hem of her T-shirt. It took all of his willpower not to slide his palm up higher.

Her hand slipped up to his shoulder. Fingernails lightly scraped the side of his neck then pushed into his hair. His racing heart jumped gears. He wrapped an arm around her, pulling her against his aroused body.

She tensed. "The steak needs to be turned over," she said, ducking her head. "Or it'll burn."

The meat was sizzling like crazy and he hadn't heard it. He let her go and watched her flip the T-bone. As soon as his body calmed down he mentally kicked himself. Kissing her was not keeping his distance. Neither was staring at her ass while she bent over to check the food in the oven.

What a goddamn fool he was. One hundred percent certified prime idiot.

He walked to the cabinet under the sink, fished out the list of chores from the wastebasket and stuck the paper back under the fridge magnet.

"After supper we'll go over your share of the chores," he said without looking at her. "Better set your alarm, sweetheart. You'll have to get up early."

# 7

SHELBY WAS OUT of bed and dressed before the alarm went off at six. It wasn't a hardship since she'd been awake for a while. Embarrassed over last night's misstep, she hadn't slept well.

God. She'd actually kissed Trent. More proof that she was insane. Not at all herself.

While technically *he'd* kissed her, she sure hadn't objected. Or resisted. In fact, she'd fully participated. No matter how she tried to spin things, that was the truth.

Pausing with her hand on the doorknob, she listened to him moving around, then heard the quiet sound of kitchen noises. She really hoped she was right. If he was in the kitchen, she could make a dash to the bathroom without running into him. She wasn't quite up to that yet.

Trent probably wasn't, either. After the kiss his mood had changed. He'd been plain grumpy. She got it. She did. When she was scared, she did a lot of things that she wouldn't do normally. Like kiss him. And think about what he'd look like without those worn jeans.

Him calling her sweetheart pretty much told her that he'd also realized the kiss had been a mistake.

Looking back, it might've been wiser for her to have

taken the bait and made herself scarce. Instead they'd gone ahead and eaten dinner together, mostly in uncomfortable silence and very quickly. Then when she'd tried to escape to her room, he'd insisted on going over her list of chores. Today she would learn how to milk a cow. Lucky her.

She made it to the bathroom without seeing him. Hurriedly finished her business, and then let the aroma of coffee lead her to the kitchen and the inevitable.

He was standing at the sink, steaming mug in hand, peering out the window. A faded navy blue T-shirt stretched across his broad shoulders.

"Good morning," she said, after taking a second to admire how his jeans hugged his butt. Dammit. Before he turned, her gaze skittered to the coffeepot. Beside it was a yellow floral cup she hoped was meant for her.

"Help yourself, if you drink coffee." He gave her frayed jeans a brief look. "Otherwise there's tea in the pantry. Milk in the fridge."

"Thanks."

The sugar was sitting out. Organic sugar, according to the bag. She didn't know why that surprised her. No reason Trent wouldn't be as health conscious as the next person.

She poured her coffee, skipped all the other stuff. Her first sip improved her disposition, as had Trent's neutral tone of voice. She was totally okay with them pretending the kiss had never happened. She only hoped he hadn't gotten the wrong idea. Because she wasn't needy and certainly would never barter herself in order to stay on the ranch. But he didn't know her, and no telling how he'd interpreted her actions. All she could really do was make sure it never happened again.

"How's the thumb?"

"Not bad." He'd stared down at it. "I should probably take off the gauze."

"Your work gloves might irritate the burn."

He snorted a laugh. "Too bad. A ranch doesn't run itself. I'd have to be half dead to take a day off, and then I'd still have to feed and water the animals."

Knowing that was added strictly for her benefit, she tried not to roll her eyes.

"I'll be in the barn," he said as he topped off his mug. "Come when you're ready."

"Are we feeding the chickens first?"

"No." He took a hasty sip. "Violet will take care of them. I'm going to show you how to milk Daisy."

"You named the cow? How adorable."

He sighed with disgust. "No, I did not name the cow," he said. "My six-year-old niece decided to call her Daisy and—it just sorta stuck." He pulled the door open. "I wouldn't mention it to people around here. They'll laugh you out of town."

Shelby pressed her lips together and nodded, not trusting herself to speak. Under all his bluster, Trent was a softie. He was very lucky she wouldn't tattle on him.

After several more gulps, she refilled her mug and headed to the barn with it. In the far back Trent had set out a pair of buckets near a weird-looking wooden contraption. She heard a pitiful bleating sound coming from behind the stacked bales in the corner and walked over to investigate.

Shelby gasped with delight. "Oh, my God, you didn't tell me you had a calf."

"Don't get attached. She's being picked up this afternoon."

"Why?"

"Because I sold her, that's why. We have too damn many females around here as it is," he muttered.

"Oh, sweetie, are you gonna miss your mama?" Shelby moved a bit closer to the narrow stall. "Is that mean man separating you from her?"

Several yards away, Trent grunted. "Yeah, you'd do a great job running a ranch."

The little one seemed curious at first. Then let out a frightened *mawww* and backed away. Shelby wondered what type of treat would be safe to give her. Either she'd ask Violet or look it up online. She wouldn't ask Trent. Leaving the calf in peace, she went over to where the "mean man" was waiting for her. "Who told you that's what I wanted to do?"

He looked up from positioning one of the buckets and frowned. "What else would you do with the Eager Beaver?"

"I want a place that's peaceful and quiet and inspiring where I can work."

"Making jewelry?"

"Yes."

"Can't you do that anywhere? You were working in Denver, right?"

"Have you ever lived in a city?"

"Just outside of Dallas. Close enough to count."

"On a ranch?"

He nodded slowly.

"Go into the city much?"

"Hell no," he said, his voice trailing off when he must've realized he'd helped make her point.

For good measure she said, "Then you should get it." She turned away when he'd stared too long and hard at her. There was something about him that made her feel vulnerable. As if with a look he could unearth her deepest secrets. "Anyway, you have to admit, the Eager Beaver isn't much of a ranch."

"Hey, hold on there—"

"Come on, Trent. You have a cow, some chickens, a dog and a couple of horses. Not exactly a ranching empire."

"Not just horses... I have American quarter horses," he

said, looking insulted. "Two of them. And Solomon has already won two races."

She stared back. "Why is it okay to name horses and not cows?"

His gaze narrowed. "You're kidding, right?"

"No. Enlighten me."

"It's different."

"Obviously." She truly didn't understand. "But what makes it different?"

"You're trying to get out of milking Dai—the cow," he said, jabbing a finger at her. "Won't happen."

He was wrong but she didn't bother correcting him. Instead she watched him scoop some grain into one of the buckets and then set it in front of the wooden thing that looked like some sort of torture device.

A moment later he led Daisy out from somewhere in the back of the barn. "You'll want to put her in this head catch while you milk her."

"Won't that hurt her?"

"Of course not. Watch."

Daisy had no problem with the setup. She dove into the grain with relish.

Trent turned the second bucket over closer to her hind end before bringing out a medium-size pail from a cabinet. "I'll show you what to do, then you try it."

She watched him as he sat on the overturned bucket, strategically placed the steel pail, grabbed a teat and started squeezing. Milk streamed into the pail. It looked simple enough but Shelby was willing to admit she was nervous. What if she hurt Daisy?

"Can you see what I'm doing?"

Shelby nodded.

"Ready to give it a try?"

"I think so," she said in a stupidly girly voice.

Trent rose and stepped back. "Better hurry before she finishes her grain."

Taking a deep breath, Shelby sat on the bucket.

"Now, squeeze the top of the teat, then close the rest of your fingers down on it one at a time and tug gently."

She did exactly what he told her to do. And nothing happened.

"Don't worry. It takes some practice. Keep trying."

Her next attempt produced a few drops. She looked up to see Trent grinning. "I can't do it with you watching."

"I want to make sure she doesn't kick you."

Shelby half whined, half whimpered.

"Here," he said, laughing. "I'll help you." She started to get to her feet, but he said, "No, stay right there."

After some jockeying for a suitable position, Trent crouched behind her. She turned to see what he was doing and the stubble on his chin grazed her cheek. He needed a shave, yet he smelled good.

"Stay facing Daisy," he said quietly, and put his arms around Shelby so that her back was pressed to his chest. "Give me your hands."

Her heart took a giant leap. "Is this really necessary?"

"Put out your hands."

She did as he asked, unclear as to his intentions. Was he trying to scare her off? Show her the kiss hadn't affected him in the least? More likely, he hadn't given it a second thought.

His palms were tough and calloused but less so than she'd expected. He guided her to the top of the teat, and then closed his large hands over her much smaller ones. "This is the amount of pressure you want to use," he said. "Can you feel what I mean?"

Oh, she felt something, all right. Tingling. Excitement. His body heat. His lips against her hair. She was wrong of course, about that part, and wrong to feel the sudden longing to repeat last night's kiss.

She really was losing it.

"Shelby?" He leaned back slightly. "You okay?"

"Fine." For heaven's sake, she'd been lounging against him as if he was a chair. Straightening, she cleared her throat. "I had a leg cramp."

"Need to walk it out?"

"No. Let's finish this."

He said nothing, but she felt the vibration of his silent laughter, reminding her how irritating he could be.

She tried to relax and let him guide her hands but it just wasn't happening. "You know what," she said, struggling to her feet, not caring if she knocked him over. "I think I'll do better without you helping. No offense."

Trent's little smirk was deliberate, or she'd eat her new Gucci purse. "You sure about that?"

"No." She smiled. Let him guess if she meant on both counts. "But I'm willing to try. I bet you have more important things to do."

He folded his arms across his chest, his boots planted a couple of feet apart. The stance seemed to narrow his waist and broaden his shoulders. He probably knew it and stood like that on purpose.

"I said, go."

"In a minute. I just want to watch you get started."

Shelby huffed. "Well, make yourself useful and get me a second pail so I won't have to get up."

His eyebrows rose. "While I appreciate your optimism, I doubt that'll be a problem." He dropped his arms to his sides. "Look, if she doesn't give you much milk, don't worry about it. Milking takes practice and Daisy can be prickly. And do not try to milk her from the back."

"Got it."

His hesitation was beginning to unnerve her.

Finally, he made a move to leave. "I'll be in the kitchen or the stable." He rubbed his arms as he turned to go. "It's kind of chilly this morning."

While he'd barely looked at her, something made her glance down at her T-shirt. And see her tightened nipples straining against the stretchy fabric.

TRENT HAD JUST put on a second pot of coffee and was debating rescuing Shelby when he heard the screen door open. He didn't blame her for giving up early. Daisy could be stubborn as all get-out. But he'd give Shelby some grief, anyway. He turned just as she set two full pails of milk on the kitchen counter.

"I wasn't sure if I should keep going. Daisy finished her grain and was getting antsy so I stopped."

Once he got past the shock he nodded. "Violet helped you."

"Excuse me." She frowned, looking insulted. "I haven't seen Violet since the day I arrived. Like you said, it wasn't hard. Daisy just needed a pep talk."

He eyed the pails. Okay, she deserved to be a little smug. "Glad it was easy. That's your chore from now on."

Some of the smugness slipped. But she nodded. "So, do you have pitchers? I assume this goes in the fridge?"

"Keep what you want and give the rest to Violet." He thought a moment. Yeah, he really needed for Violet to bend her ear. "I'll take it to her later."

Shelby grinned. "Afraid she'll tell me all your secrets?"

"If you think I'd let that old busybody know anything about me, you're out of your mind."

"Oh, that's probably true," she said, sighing. Then she studied Trent, her eyes even more green with the sunlight flooding in through the window. "You like her."

"Who?"

"You do," Shelby said matter-of-factly. "And she likes you. It's nice."

He frowned at the slight wistfulness in her voice. "Not that nice. Wait until you've been around a while," he said, and refilled his mug. "Now, what's that smile for?"

She walked over to him, and he got a bit itchy until he saw she only wanted coffee. "Good to know you haven't packed my bags and loaded my car."

He shouldn't have felt disappointed. What had he expected? Another kiss? Right, as if the first one hadn't been a dumb mistake. Damn, he wished he could forget how sweet she'd tasted. Forget the softness and warmth of her body pressed against him. Two nights in a row now, he hadn't slept for thinking about her.

"Look, when I said wait till you've been around awhile, I meant until your belongings are delivered. We should know who owns the Eager Beaver by then." Was it his imagination or was she struggling to keep a straight face? "As soon as you redirect the movers, you can hit the road. Better yet, leave me a forwarding address. I'd be happy to take care of it for you."

"Maybe I should just call the moving company now."

"Excellent idea."

"Dream on." She tore off a paper towel and wiped a spill on the counter. "Trash? Under the sink, right?" She opened the lower cabinet and frowned. "You have a leak."

"Gee, what was your first clue?" Maybe he should kiss her again. Just to shut her up. "I know there's a problem. Why do you think I put a bowl under there?"

"This might sound silly, but you could…oh, I don't know—" she moved a shoulder, tilted her head to the side "—maybe fix it instead?"

Trent ground his molars together. "It's gonna take some time. I'm not a plumber."

She dropped to a crouch and moved the wastebasket to

the side. "It looks fairly straightforward. Shouldn't take much."

"Be my guest."

After poking around she asked, "You have a wrench?" When he didn't respond, she looked up. "Just bring me your toolbox."

He was more than happy to call her bluff. By the time he returned with three different size wrenches—with the toolbox sitting outside the kitchen door just in case—he wasn't surprised that she'd disappeared.

The cabinet door had been left open, the wastebasket set aside. The half-filled bowl hadn't been moved. He thought for a moment, trying to decide if he should go ahead and tackle the job since he had the tools out. If he screwed up, his neighbor four miles down would bail him out. For a kid, Jimmy was fairly handy with this sort of thing and he owed Trent big time for helping him move cattle. Actually, the guy wasn't that young, maybe twenty-five, six years younger than Trent. But somehow Jimmy managed to make him feel old.

"Oh, good." Shelby walked in wearing a different T-shirt, with a faded green towel draped over her arm. Her bed-tousled hair was now pulled into a ponytail. He'd liked it better before.

"I figured you'd skipped out," he said.

"I told you I'd fix it."

"Yep, you did. Here you go." He passed her the wrenches and couldn't help noticing that the new shirt was tighter, stained and sported a few small holes.

She laid the wrenches on the linoleum, then spread the towel next to it.

"Would you like a pillow, too?"

"Oh God." She rolled her eyes as she lowered herself to the floor. "You're going to be one of those guys, aren't you?"

"What?"

"Get all macho and then pissy over a woman show-ing you up."

"Hell no. I want it fixed. And someone else doing the work is right up my alley." He folded his arms across his chest. "Assuming that someone knows what they're doing."

"Yeah?" She smiled. "Watch and learn…sweetheart."

The worn T-shirt was a size too small for her. And dis-tracting as hell. But he wasn't comfortable leaving yet.

Something unpleasant had just occurred to him. Three months ago he'd installed the garbage disposal himself after watching a DIY video online. So far so good, but knowing she'd be tinkering under there was making him nervous.

"Tell you what, Shelby, I'll take care of the leak this af-ternoon." He watched her lie back, then do a little shimmy as she tried to get in a suitable position. "Before dinner."

"That's okay. I'm here."

He was probably worried for nothing. If it was going to come loose it would've done so already. His gaze lingered on her hips as he waited for the next little wiggle.

"I thought you had chores to do," she muttered, her voice muffled from partway inside the cabinet.

"Right after I finish my coffee." Where was his mug, anyway? He turned and saw it on the counter near the stove. After replacing the cold brew he resumed his post.

"Wow, this pipe is old." With her arms stretched back, the shirt's worn fabric cupped her breasts. "And stubborn."

He refrained from commenting, too busy watching her and thinking things he shouldn't be thinking.

A thud cut him off. Metal clanged against metal.

"Shelby?" He dropped to his haunches, sloshing coffee everywhere, including her jeans.

"What?"

"You okay?"

"Fine. I told you, it's this old pipe…" She muttered a curse. "Why are you still here?"

This was his house and he'd leave when he was darned good and ready. She shifted, giving him a glimpse of smooth toned belly just below her navel. His splashed coffee had gotten her T-shirt. A wet spot had spread across her hardened left nipple.

Trent shot to his feet. "I'll be outside. Watch out for the disposal. I put it in myself."

# 8

By MIDAFTERNOON SHELBY was disappointed that she hadn't seen Trent. Having fixed the leak, she'd wanted to gloat. Nothing too obnoxious. Just a smug nod of her head would be fun. Or a perfectly intoned "well, yeah." She'd even decided she might not be above a plain "duh."

Although, the reason he'd made himself scarce was most likely to avoid her. So, no, she'd keep her mouth shut. Her trip to town had confirmed her worst fear about the Eager Beaver. Her inheritance was worthless. Of all the stupid times to have acted impulsively. Returning to Denver wasn't an option.

Her gaze automatically went to her cell where it sat charging on the nightstand. She hadn't checked it once this morning. She'd lost count of Donald's texts and voice mails. It wasn't as if she would never speak to him again. She just wasn't ready yet. In truth, there was little left to say. But she'd return his calls at some point. If only to make certain he understood it was over between them.

She sat on the edge of her bed and sighed at the grime she'd had little luck removing from under her fingernails. Between living out here and making her own jewelry, no more manicures for her. She wouldn't miss them. Just like she hadn't missed her luxurious studio at Williamson Jewelers.

Oh, she'd gotten used to having her mini-fridge stocked with mineral water, diet sodas and fruit juices. Anything she or a client consumed was replaced overnight. It wasn't something she'd miss, though, not like daily lunch delivery and having her dry cleaning picked up in the morning and hung behind her door that same afternoon, if she wanted. Mrs. Williamson had made it clear from the beginning that Shelby's sole focus was to be on her exclusive designs and the super-rich customers who paid outrageous prices for them.

One week Shelby had been a struggling college student about to graduate and hoping to get a job in marketing. The next thing she knew she'd been swept into the posh and glamorous world of Tad and Anastasia Williamson. They'd been nice, if a bit too reserved, though not in their effusive praise of her work. Their job offer had come with a salary so huge Shelby had been speechless. Something they'd mistaken for hesitancy and tacked on more money.

Eight months later she'd met their son Donald, a prominent Denver attorney. She couldn't say it was love at first sight, but with his good looks and smooth moves, her head had turned plenty. At heart, Donald wasn't a bad person. It simply had never occurred to him that the world truly did not revolve around the Williamsons. His class-conscious mother was mostly at fault. But Donald was a bright guy. It was past time he figured it out.

For Shelby the dream had begun five years ago. But she had never belonged in that world. Turned out her large salary hadn't gone far at all. With the Williamsons, it was all about image, and that had cost Shelby plenty, both emotionally and financially. She really should've woken up long before last week.

She stared at the box containing her supplies. Tempted as

she was to unpack them, the timing was wrong. She needed a large, well-lit, ventilated space to work. Trent would have heart failure if she took over the living room. She doubted fixing the sink had earned her that much grace.

Since she'd finished some light housekeeping, she changed from her old work T-shirt to a more flattering turquoise cotton knit. Next she planned on making dinner, glad she wasn't a messy cook. She hoped that was still true. It had been a while…

She went to the fridge and took out the hamburger she'd bought in town yesterday. Trent's meager assortment of spices and herbs was pitiful but she'd make do. She found a mixing bowl and baking pan, and everything else she needed to put together a decent meatloaf.

If Trent had plans for dinner, that was okay. But he'd shared his steak with her so she figured it was her turn. The view of the Rockies from the kitchen window was really amazing.

The late afternoon sun had sunk behind the peaks, leaving behind clouds that looked like wisps of pink cotton candy. She thought about running to get her phone so she could take a picture but got distracted.

Shelby wasn't sure how she'd missed him at first. Trent was in the corral working with a reddish-brown horse, his focus completely centered on the beautiful animal. Anyone half blind could see that Trent was in his element. For him, the rest of the world seemed to have disappeared. Spellbound, she could barely drag her gaze away. But if she worked quickly…

While waiting for the oven to preheat, she peeled and cut up potatoes, then put them in a pot to boil. Once the meatloaf was in the oven, she calculated how much time she had before she needed to turn the stove off, then walked outside. If she was intruding, she'd know right away. One good thing about Trent, she thought wryly, he didn't hold back.

She'd been leaning against the corral for almost five minutes before he even noticed her. His fleeting frown told her nothing. He tugged down the brim of his hat and led the horse toward her. Her racing heart made sense when she flashed back to the excitement of her first pony ride. A time when things had still been okay between her parents. She must've been about nine.

"Am I interrupting?" she asked, her gaze glued to the muscled horse. "If so I'll leave."

"For good?"

Okay, she'd laid the welcome mat out for that. "What's his name?"

"Solomon." Trent stroked the horse's neck. "This is Shelby," he told the animal. "How do you greet a lady?"

Solomon went down on his front legs and bowed.

Surprised and delighted, Shelby giggled like a silly schoolgirl. "What kind is he?"

Trent's smile vanished in a second. "A quarter horse," he said, clearly insulted.

"Ah, right. You mentioned that before. Sorry."

"Damn straight. Everybody knows the American quarter horse is the best all-purpose breed in the world," he said with a brief self-mocking smile. "They're used for rodeos, barrel-racing, steer roping, pleasure rides, ranch work. As for racing? They can turn more quickly and accelerate faster than any other horse." He gave Solomon a fond smile. "You've won a couple races yourself, haven't you, buddy?"

The horse moved his head in a vague nod.

Shelby let out a short laugh. "He's amazing. May I pet him?"

"Sure." Trent brought the horse closer.

"He's smaller than I expected."

"Don't let that fool you. Quarter horses generally are more compact. But they're powerful sprinters, agile and well-balanced. That's partly what makes them so versatile."

"You're so handsome." With a tentative hand, she stroked the side of Solomon's neck just as she'd seen Trent do.

"No need to be afraid. He likes you. See how his ears are pricked forward. If he didn't like you touching him you'd know it."

"Kind of like his owner." She realized that hadn't come out right when Trent raised a brow at her. "No, not— I meant the part about him not holding back."

With a little smile betraying his amusement, he lifted his hat and resettled it on his head. "You take care of that leak?"

"All done."

His expression said it all. He hadn't expected that outcome.

Shelby grinned. "Don't look so surprised. I'm very resourceful."

"I don't doubt it. But I figured you would've come out gloating."

"Oh, I thought about it. I even practiced what I was going to say while I did some tidying up."

His gaze narrowed. "You cleaned, too?"

She stopped petting Solomon and held up both hands. "I didn't touch any of your personal stuff."

"I wasn't worried about that. Can you cook?"

"Depends. What's it worth to you?"

"Are you serious? I'm already giving you bathroom and kitchen privileges."

"Well, aren't you just a knight in shining armor?"

Solomon snorted.

"Yes, I know, handsome. But we'll just ignore him," Shelby said, and went back to stroking his neck.

This time Trent snorted. "You'll never turn him against me."

He sounded so serious she had to laugh. "It just so happens I made dinner." The reminder had her checking her watch.

"Real food? Not chef's salad or quiche or anything like that."

"Oh, no." Shelby tried her best to look disappointed. "You don't like quiche?"

He cleared his throat. "It's okay."

"Good." She gave him a bright smile. "Dinner will be ready in thirty minutes. See you later, handsome." She gave the horse an extra pat, then hurried toward the house before she burst out laughing.

"Do I HAVE time for a shower?" Trent entered by the back door twenty-five minutes later. "Or is that gonna ruin the quiche?"

By the time Shelby looked up from the salad she was tossing, he was sniffing the air, his brows drawn together in a suspicious frown. "No, go ahead," she told him.

"What's that smell?"

"Meatloaf."

He hung his hat on a wall peg, a faint smile curving his mouth as he walked out of the kitchen.

Shelby grinned, too, but didn't let him see. Figuring she had a spare ten minutes she decided to make gravy for the mashed potatoes. It had been her favorite comfort food as a kid, and even in college, mostly because it was a cheap dish. But it'd been years since she'd indulged. Thanksgiving dinner with the Williamsons was always a gourmet affair—no mashed potatoes and gravy.

Deciding to go all out, fat and calories be damned, she pulled out butter along with the other necessary ingredients.

She repeated the earlier ritual of searching cabinets and drawers, this time for a whisk and the right size pot. Before she actually started on the gravy, her cell buzzed.

Dread slithered down her spine. Her good mood fizzled. It was probably Donald again. She owed him another conversation, she knew that. Something made her grab the phone instead of letting it go to voice mail. She frowned at the caller ID. Wasn't it kind of late in Germany?

"Hi, Mom, is everything okay?"

"You tell me."

Shelby briefly closed her eyes and rubbed her temple. *Wait for it. Any second now...*

On cue, her mother let out a long-suffering sigh. "What on earth is wrong with you, Shelby Ann?"

She knew, Shelby thought, but how? Her mother had never called her at work, only on her cell. And very seldom. "Nothing's wrong. I'm terrific. Never felt better."

"Not according to Donald."

She pulled a chair away from the table and sat down. "Donald?" she murmured, the smell of meatloaf making her stomach turn. "You called him?"

"No, of course not. How would I know his number? Donald called me."

That made even less sense. They hadn't met yet. "What did he want?" she asked calmly.

"How could you be so stupid?"

Shelby flinched, though it wasn't the first time she'd been called that by her mom. It shouldn't still hurt. "Do you even want to know why I broke the engagement?"

"Do you honestly think you can do better?" Gloria's voice had risen. "He's an attorney. He's rich. His family is rich. He'll inherit everything one day. Don't you understand how lucky you were to find a man like him? A man who wants to marry you and not just keep you on the side?"

"Oh, Mom, please." Shelby let out a sigh that sounded depressingly like her mother's.

"Lord knows I tried my best with you, Shelby. I did.

With no help from your worthless father, I might add. But you—"

"Mom, stop. Just stop."

Silence lasted only seconds. "Where are you?"

"Montana." The word slipped out before Shelby had a chance to think. No one needed to know where she was.

"Montana? Why? What could you possibly expect to—" Gloria paused, then huffed out a breath. "It doesn't matter. Donald hasn't given up on you. It's not too late. He wants you back."

"Tough."

"What did you say?"

"I am not going back to Denver or Donald or my job. There will be no wedding. I don't know how to say it any simpler." Knots of tension cramped her shoulders. A small insistent headache had begun to throb near her temple. "And you need to stay out of it. Are we clear?"

"What happened, baby?" Now came the cloyingly sweet conciliatory tone her mom had decided made her sound maternal. "Did he have a small fling? Men stray from time to time. It's a fact of life. Certainly not a reason to cancel the wedding."

"I have to go. We'll talk again soon."

"But, honey—"

"Goodbye, Mom."

For the first time in her life, Shelby hung up on her mother.

She dropped the phone on the table, then dropped her chin to her chest, waiting for guilt to set in. She felt pretty good, actually. Her shoulders and head not so much. Her eyes were moist but no tears had fallen. That was progress.

God, she was almost twenty-eight. A grown woman who'd supported herself since she was eighteen. How could she still let Gloria get to her? Shelby had already predicted her mom's reaction. Nothing new there. She hadn't even met Donald yet she was rallying to his side.

Okay, that part was hard to take.

Shelby breathed in deeply, trying to dislodge the lump blocking her air passage.

Well, so much for dinner. Everything but the gravy was made. At least Trent could eat. Her stomach couldn't take any food. Still, she would never recommend the *Gloria diet*.

She pushed to her feet, anxious for the safety of her room. The meal was warm enough. If not, Trent was a big boy. He could figure it out.

The gravy ingredients were scattered on the counter. The thought of putting everything away made her want to weep. But she couldn't just leave it. Exhausted suddenly, she took a step and, from the corner of her eye, caught a glimpse of Trent.

Wearing a clean T-shirt, his hair damp, he stood in the doorway. For how long was anyone's guess. Judging by his expression, he'd heard plenty.

TRENT WAS AT a loss. The second he'd figured out she was on her cell he should've made himself scarce.

"Hey, good timing. Dinner's ready." Shelby forced a quick smile, then couldn't turn away fast enough. "I have this stupid headache or I would've made gravy. Should I leave out the stuff for you, or put everything away?"

"Leave it."

She cleared her throat. "So, the salad is done. I made a simple dressing. It's in the fridge. Don't feel obligated—it won't hurt my feelings if you don't like Italian," she said with her back to him while washing and drying her hands. "Please, go ahead and eat. I'll have something later after I get rid of this headache."

He didn't know Shelby well, but it was obvious she was

uncomfortable. The smart thing for him to do was pretend he'd forgotten something outside. Let her have her privacy until she could escape to her room.

But he knew a little of what she might be going through, and he'd feel like shit if he just did the easy thing.

"Shelby?"

"Huh?" If she continued drying her hands she wouldn't have any skin left.

"I overheard part of your conversation. I'm sorry for that."

She turned slowly to face him. "What did you hear?" No tears, but her eyes were misty, more sad than embarrassed.

If he made her cry he'd kick himself into next month. "I know you were engaged and now you're not."

She smiled a little. "Is that a stab at diplomacy?"

Trent sighed, wishing he'd just walked on outside. "Look, you know I'm divorced, and no, it doesn't make me an expert on breakups. But I wanted to say that it might feel like the end of the world right now, but it gets easier if not better. And take it easy on yourself. Respect the grieving period, but remember there's still life on the other side." He shrugged. "Whatever happens, trust your instincts. That's how animals survive. We could learn a lot from them." Something he needed to get through his thick skull, himself.

Shelby nodded, but was giving him the oddest look. Probably hadn't expected him to be so talkative. That made two of them.

"Ending the engagement was for the best. It was scary at first, but a huge relief, too. I'm good with my decision," she said. "I honestly am okay. It's just—" Her voice cracked and she looked away. "I need to lie down for a bit. It's this headache—"

Head down, she started for the door to the living room.

He stepped aside to let her pass, and was surprised when she stopped to put a hand on his arm.

"Thank you," she said softly.

"No problem." He hadn't really done anything. So he'd fessed up to overhearing her phone conversation. As for the advice, normally he was the last person he'd listen to. But he knew something about the pain of lost love.

"I mean it. Thanks." She leaned in and kissed his cheek.

His arms came up around her. Not planned. It was the worst possible thing he could do. So he tried to mitigate the situation by patting her back.

Shelby looped her arms around his neck and gave him a light squeeze. Her soft breasts pressing against his chest had his body responding before he could order himself to heel. Luckily she retreated before discovering the flag had been raised.

He plowed a hand through his damp hair, hoping to keep her attention directed above his chest. "I don't mind waiting to eat."

"No, please, don't wait." She smiled, but it wasn't her usual. The woman could light the whole house without electricity when she wanted.

"Hey, listen," he said as she turned. "Tomorrow we should set up a place where you can work on your jewelry."

She blinked. "That might be premature," she said cautiously. "Don't you think?"

"No, not necessarily." He understood what she was getting at, and he hoped he wasn't being a first-class sucker. "How about we make a deal? Right now. No matter what happens with the Eager Beaver, no matter who holds the winning ticket, the other person has a grace period, two or three months before they have to clear out—whatever you think is fair. What do you say?"

She studied him a moment. "You don't have to be nice to me."

Trent laughed.

"I meant extra nice because of what you heard back there." She made a vague gesture. "I'm really fine."

"I believe you. Do we have a deal?"

She bit at her lip which made him want to forget the whole thing. "How about three months?"

"Three months," he agreed.

Reluctantly he accepted the hand she'd extended, knowing full well this agreement came with a catch. This woman was going to have him tied up in a hundred knots. More like a thousand if they lasted the entire three months. Knowing what he did now, he couldn't touch her again. No matter how tempting.

She might think everything was okay, but based on his own experience, the shock might not have worn off yet. He seriously doubted she knew how she felt and he wasn't about to get caught in the middle of anything.

# 9

"GET YOUR LAZY ass out of the way." Trent waited for the dog to move. Mutt barely lifted his head then settled in a more comfortable position in the loose hay. "Why aren't you bothering Shelby? I thought she was your new best friend."

Mutt continued to ignore him.

Trent leaned the pitchfork against the barn wall and yanked off his hat. The temperature was too warm for September. Course in a matter of weeks he'd be looking over his shoulder for the first sign of snow and griping about that.

Since making the deal with Shelby two days ago, everything seemed to irritate him. He knew the cause. And it wasn't the fourteen-hour days he'd been working. The look-but-don't-touch vow he'd made to himself seemed to be hanging over his head like a rain cloud ready to burst. It didn't make any sense because nothing had changed since day one. He was through with women. Not with sex, just emotional involvement.

The part where you laid your heart on the line never knowing when it would get trampled. Uncomplicated sex was the way to go.

Someday soon he'd dip his bucket in the well again. But it wouldn't be anywhere close to home. And not with a woman who had any expectations beyond a satisfying few hours in bed. Or a woman who was on the rebound. That could get sticky.

Another thing irking him was Violet's radio silence. She had practically pulled a disappearing act. She hadn't been sitting on her porch or coming out to collect eggs and making wisecracks. It had gotten so bad that he'd worried she was sick and knocked on her door two days ago. She'd about taken his head off for disturbing her television program.

While he was relieved her health appeared okay, he couldn't help worrying that she was either up to no good or knew something about the Eager Beaver she wasn't anxious to reveal. By the time the horses were fed, the idea of checking on her again wouldn't let him be. Something was on that old lady's mind, and dammit, he didn't need any more surprises.

Leaving Mutt to soak up the sun, Trent headed over to the double-wide. Expecting to hear himself being called every name in the book, he knocked. Violet swung the door open and said, "'Bout time you came by. What if I'd had a heart attack or something?"

She moved back to let him in. A very rare experience that made him even more nervous. He shook his head as he passed her into the living room. The trailer had all the standard conveniences, along with a big plasma TV, and was neat as a pin.

"Now you know I won't worry about that," he said. "Seeing as how you've told me yourself you don't have a heart."

She gave him a wicked look. "For the next five minutes you are to keep your mouth shut, you hear me?"

"What are you talking about? Jesus, it smells like smoke in here. Don't you ever open any windows?"

"Okay, you're just eating up your minutes, and if you keep it up, you're not gonna hear something that you ought."

"Fine," he said, his heart beating fast, and not from secondhand smoke. Dammit. She did know something. But if she knew the Eager Beaver was his, she would have said already. On the other hand, when had Violet done anything the easy way.

"You gotta swear on your great-granddaddy's grave that what I'm about to tell you is just between us. That means you don't call your momma or tell your friends or your… houseguest. You can talk to me, but that's it."

"Okay, now I'm worried. Did you fall and hit your head?"

"Shush, I'm telling you something. Swear now. Right now, that you won't say a word 'bout this to anyone."

"Okay, okay. I swear."

"The Eager Beaver is yours. And in two weeks, I'll have what I need to prove it."

The double-wide seemed to sway. "What? How? Why in two weeks?"

Violet glared at him. "Because that's how long it'll take me to get the paperwork."

Trent didn't like this, didn't like it one bit. "You mean the deed?"

"I ain't saying no more about it." Violet got that stubborn glint in her eye that always meant trouble. "Now, get out of here. My shows are coming on."

Two hours and two phone calls later, Trent still couldn't make heads or tails out of the situation. His mom had barely set foot in the door after returning from her trip when he'd called to see if she'd been to the bank yet. She must've sensed his panic because she checked their safe deposit box and got back to him in thirty minutes. Turned out Violet was a trustee of some kind. Legally. According to a handwritten document that had been notarized. That was all his mother could find. What in the hell had his great-granddad been thinking? If Trent didn't end up with an ulcer before this mess got straightened out it would be a damn miracle.

It was Mutt that pulled him out of his swirling thoughts. The dog raised his head, ears perked.

Seconds later Trent heard an engine and stuck his head out of the barn. It was his neighbor. Jimmy parked his four-wheeler behind Shelby's car and then circled the sedan, checking out the chrome wheels.

"You got some fancy company?" he asked when he saw Trent.

"Not exactly." Of all the times for Jimmy to come by. Instead of being the happiest man in Salina County that his home still belonged to him, Trent had been doing some thinking. Having thoughts he shouldn't be bothered with. Like how Shelby was gonna take the news, and how they'd just gotten to a real civil place but that was tricky, too. And now, Jimmy.

"What's going on?" he asked, as much to himself as to his company.

"Dad and Cal are busy sorting and weighing calves." Jimmy gave the car a final once-over before joining Trent outside the barn. "Any chance you can help me with weaning vaccinations?"

Trent eyed the younger man. He was a tall husky guy, much like his brother Cal, only Jimmy wasn't sure he wanted to stick around and be a rancher. He had a long list of chores he hated, all of them relating to cattle, something which he and Trent had in common.

"You can't do that by yourself?" Trent said, figuring

there was more to Jimmy's request. "You wouldn't be doing some branding now, would you?"

Jimmy's wry grin confirmed Trent's suspicion.

"Nope. No way." Trent peeled off a glove. "You know how much I hate branding."

"Well, me, too."

"Yeah, too bad. Talk your dad into breeding horses."

"Come on, Kimball. We'll hit the Watering Hole afterward. All the beer you can drink on me."

"Nope." Trent bent over to pick up Mutt's water bowl. He liked Jimmy, and he even felt for the guy. Growing up on a ranch in a place as isolated as Blackfoot Falls with limited skills, his options were few. He could end up staying on the family ranch for the rest of his life.

"Holy shit. Who is that?"

Trent didn't have to turn around to know who Jimmy meant. "Keep your mouth open like that and you'll be coughing up flies for a week."

Jimmy finally closed his mouth but he didn't move, just kept staring. "Come on, who is she?"

Trent turned, curious whether Shelby could see them. She was standing on the porch wearing her normal work clothes—tight faded jeans, ripped in several places and a white T-shirt. This one wasn't as snug as some of the others. But it didn't hide anything, either.

"That's Shelby," he said, still not sure if she'd seen them. "Quit staring like a jackass."

"Is she yours?"

"Jesus." Trent laughed, shook his head. "You have about as much chance with her as you have of getting me to help you brand calves."

Jimmy patted down his curly blond hair. It had a tendency to stick out. Like now. "Call her over. Introduce us."

"You're barking up the wrong tree, kid."

Shelby shaded her eyes and searched the cloudless sky.

Hoping to spot a hawk, he imagined. She loved watching them wheel and soar. Occasionally she'd catch sight of an eagle, and get as excited as a five-year-old on Christmas morning. She stepped off the porch and went straight for the double-wide.

Seeing her got Mutt up and moving. Tail wagging, he chased after her. She stopped to pet him, noticed them standing in the shadow of the barn, and waved.

Jimmy responded with a raised hand and a flushed face. "Don't just stand there. Ask her to come over here," he grumbled.

Trent had been hoping she wouldn't, but it was better than her knocking on Violet's door. He let out a breath when she walked toward them.

"Hello," she said, smiling at Jimmy and then glancing at Trent. "I hope I'm not interrupting."

"Nah, I came to do some arm-twisting," Jimmy said, all teeth.

Shelby grinned. "Is it working?"

"Not with the rotten mood he's in."

"Oh, I thought it was just me."

Holding in a curse, Trent looked at Mutt's water bowl and remembered he was supposed to fill it. "Shelby, this is Jimmy," Trent said, gesturing. "Jimmy…Shelby. I'm going back to work."

"Wait." Shelby caught his arm as he turned. "Where's the circuit breaker?"

"You blew a fuse?"

"I'm sure I just tripped it."

"I'll take care of it," Trent muttered, annoyed that he'd caught a whiff of her. She had no business smelling this good while she was making her jewelry. Her scent was the equivalent of an earworm. It would stick with him for the rest of the day. Shit. How was he going to hold it together when he'd have to smell her, see her, every day for three months.

"Um, you should probably show me where the box is located."

He cleared his throat. "So, you trip fuses a lot?"

She ducked her head. "I wouldn't say a lot…"

"Shoot, I'll show her where it is," Jimmy said with a sly grin for Trent. "I know you're busy."

"If you still want help with the vaccinations I'll have time later. Tomorrow I'm leaving at first light and I'll be gone all day." He felt Shelby's eyes on him. Probably because he hadn't mentioned he was going anywhere. Not that he needed her permission.

Jimmy sighed. "Still a no on the branding, huh?"

In answer, Trent grabbed the pitchfork he'd left against the wall and with the bowl, headed toward the back of the barn. A second before he was out of earshot, he heard Jimmy ask, "So, have you been to the Watering Hole yet?"

SHELBY WISHED SHE knew what was bothering Trent. She'd narrowed the list to two possibilities, neither of which she wanted to bring up. Though if he regretted agreeing to a grace period, she needed to know pretty quick.

The movers had phoned to make a delivery appointment. Thankfully the call had gone to voice mail while she was showering. She still hadn't made up her mind. Did she let them bring her belongings? Or tell them to store everything?

Storage would be the obvious choice if Blackfoot Falls had an adequate facility that allowed her access. The hardware store owner kept four containers in his storage barn available to rent. She'd checked, but they were all taken.

Getting her hands on the deed to the Eager Beaver wasn't an issue. At least in terms of taking possession of her things. She already knew all she had packed away was her grandfather's will.

Since it was getting late, she poured herself a cup of decaf, then glanced out the kitchen window. No Trent. No Violet. Not even Mutt was in sight. As far as she knew, Jimmy had left as soon as she'd gone back to work.

In spite of herself, she wondered where Trent was going in the morning. He hadn't said, though he had no reason to tell her anything about his schedule, or his life. Especially if the point of leaving tomorrow was to get away from her.

Three evenings ago, after the call from her mom, he'd wowed her with his compassion and insight. The next day? Boom. He'd become a completely different person.

He hadn't been rude, not even all that grumpy. The change was more subtle than that. He'd seemed almost… detached. A couple of times he'd mentioned fall was a busy season, and while she didn't doubt it, she recognized it was also an excuse not to engage with her.

"Hey…" The man in question strolled into the kitchen, surprising her since she'd assumed he was outside.

She saw his gaze zero in on the coffeemaker. "It's decaf."

He made a wry face.

"Columbian decaf. It's good." Oh, damn, the coffee-maker was his, and she was tying it up. She set down her mug. "I'll make a fresh pot."

"No, that's okay."

She was already opening the upper cabinet where he kept the mugs, coffee and sugar.

"I shouldn't stay up late, anyway." He lightly touched the small of her back as he reached around her to grab a mug.

The contact startled her, made her clumsy. "Right." She almost knocked over her coffee trying to slip out of his way. "You're leaving early."

"I can wait, head out around nine-thirty," he said, concentrating on his mug. "If you thought you might wanna go with—" He shook his head, frowned. "I'm saying this backward."

She didn't care. She'd heard the important part. What a relief he wasn't upset with her… "Go where?"

"Have you thought about renting a booth at the county fair?" He turned to face her and must've noticed she was confused. "To sell your jewelry."

"Huh. The fair?"

"I know you want to set up an online business but you mentioned festivals are a good place for the style you make. So, why not at a fair?"

"I don't know. I've never been… I thought a county fair would be about livestock and baking contests."

Smiling, he nodded. "It is. But there are also crafts on display and for sale. Afraid I can't be more specific." One corner of his mouth lifted a bit higher than the other. "It's been a long time since I've gone to one, myself."

She had to stop staring and concentrate on what he was saying. The sudden knowledge that she'd been starved for that smile unnerved her. Gathering her wits, she thought for a moment. A flutter of excitement flickered in her tummy.

"Yes, I want to do it." Her mind raced, collecting and cataloguing, as she started to pace. "I don't have too many pieces ready but I can— Wait. When is the fair? I can't remember. How long does it run?"

Trent was leaning against the counter, mug in hand, watching her with a curiously warm smile. Nothing like the slightly lopsided grin from a minute ago. His eyes had darkened so much they might've been brown instead of gray.

He straightened and sobered. "I should've said before getting your hopes up. It starts in a week, runs for three days but they might not have any booths left. Rent is cheap and people tend to snap 'em up. But I have a string or two I can pull."

She nodded, digesting the information and thinking back to her trip to town. The fair had been the main topic of conversation. "Only if it's not too much trouble." She kept her expression blank, not wanting any hint of disappointment to show. "Really. No big deal if it doesn't work out."

"It'll be big to me. You're really excited."

"I am," she admitted, and grabbed her mug, mostly to have something to do with her hands. "It would take a lot of preparation, so if it doesn't fly, no harm, no foul. Okay?"

"Tomorrow I'm going to see a guy about a horse he wants trained and then go have a look at a colt I'm thinking of buying. If you're interested in going with me, we can stop in town on the way back and see about signing you up for a booth."

"Tell me what time and I'll be ready."

"How does nine sound?"

"I can be ready earlier."

"No, nine is fine. It gives me plenty of time to feed the stock and hitch the trailer. I'll even buy you breakfast."

Shelby let out a squeak of joy that sounded entirely too obnoxious and loud.

Trent reared back, frowning and chuckling at once. "What was that?"

"Eating out. Someone else cooking. I'm totally in." She paused, hoping she hadn't given him the impression she resented making meals. It was only fair, after all. "Can I ask you something?"

He didn't look too keen on it. "Go ahead."

"When I broke off my engagement, it wasn't on a whim or because I didn't get my way or—"

"None of my business," he said, cutting her short and shaking his head. "I haven't given it a thought."

"I know, it's just that you haven't been yourself and since you're divorced and that might be a touchy subject…" She watched him dump the rest of his coffee in the sink and rinse the mug. Dammit, she hadn't meant to chase him away. Why had she even… "I thought you were angry with me."

"I'm not angry," he said, pausing to look her in the eyes. Then walked out of the kitchen.

She'd give anything if she could take back what she'd said. She'd never been this clumsy and awkward around anyone. So why Trent?

THE MORNINGS WERE cold enough for Trent to wear a jacket when he fed the horses at sunrise. Hard to believe when the daytime temperatures had been hovering well above normal. Since they'd be gone until late afternoon, he'd suggested to Shelby that she dress in layers. Not like she was going bobsledding.

He glanced at her, bundled up in a puffy down coat, sitting on the passenger side of his truck. "Didn't you say you lived in Denver most of your life?"

"All of it. Until a week ago." She turned to look at him. "Why?"

She'd wrapped a blue scarf around her neck and over her head and ears so that all he could see were her eyes and nose.

He chuckled. "I can adjust the heater."

"No, thanks. I'm very comfy." She pulled off one mitten and picked up her to-go mug of coffee. She'd prepared one for each of them and filled a thermos, even though he'd assured her they were only driving a hundred miles, give or take.

"I don't get it," he said. "I know for a fact Denver gets downright frigid at times."

"Yes, it does."

"It's still September, Shelby." He divided his attention between her and the road. "Look at you."

"What?" She glanced down. "I need an adjustment period between seasons," she said with a defensive lift of her chin.

"Okay. I meant no offense."

"I know." She sighed. "This coat and the mittens came out of the emergency kit I keep in my trunk. I wasn't thinking clearly when I left," she murmured and stared out the window.

He was more than happy to drop the subject. He didn't want to hear about her departure, or her engagement, or whether she was second-guessing herself. It was difficult enough thinking about his own situation. Now that he knew the ranch was his—according to Violet, at least—he'd been hard-pressed to think of anything else. The whole reason Shelby was coming along this morning was to get a booth at the fair. He didn't know what kind of money she expected to make selling her jewelry, but he figured either she'd earn enough to help her move on or she'd find out Blackfoot Falls wasn't a good place to set up shop.

Trent sure didn't want to regret bringing her along. The other day he'd learned too much about her, then said too much. Neither of them needed to forge a bond. It would make everything harder in the long run.

He was weirdly grateful they'd already agreed to the three-month grace period. Even so, he knew the news that she didn't own the ranch would crush her. He understood about last chances and chasing dreams.

Dammit, thoughts like those were exactly what he was supposed to avoid. If they were going to live together for three whole months, he had to stop thinking about her life and her dreams, and put all his energy into his own.

So what did he go and do? Put himself in a truck with her for a long drive. He'd like to think his offer was inspired by his good nature and had nothing to do with Jimmy chatting her up yesterday. The kid was too young for her. And even if he wasn't, Trent didn't care what she did.

"Oh, shoot." Her gaze was fixed on the dashboard clock. "I forgot to call the movers." She pulled off the other mitten and fumbled inside her coat pocket. "They called yesterday for a delivery appointment."

"How much stuff do you have?"

"Not a lot. My apartment was small."

He told himself to keep his mouth shut. Shelby was a grown woman. Let her figure out what to do. He checked the Exiss in the rearview mirror, mostly out of habit. The trailer was empty and it might well be returning empty. Deciding to bring it had been a tough call. He hoped it didn't make him seem too eager about buying the colt. Though this wasn't Dallas. He knew the Landers family and they'd ask a fair price.

Glancing over at Shelby, he saw the cell in her hand. She was staring at it and giving her lower lip a workout.

*None of my business*, he reminded himself and went back to concentrating on the road ahead.

A few silent minutes passed.

"The spare bedroom," he said wanting to kick himself. "And the equipment shed behind the barn. They both have extra room. The shed is solid, waterproof and airtight."

She blinked at him, then frowned slightly. "How far away is Kalispell?"

"A little less than an hour from Blackfoot Falls. Tack on another twenty minutes from the Eager Beaver."

She thumbed the small keyboard on her phone. A few minutes later she shook her head. "I still can't get online."

"Service will be spotty for the next couple of hours. You should be able to make a call, though."

"I need to know what I'm going to tell them first."

Okay, so she didn't like the spare-room-and-shed idea. Good. Made things simpler.

"What about when we stop for breakfast? Can I get online then?"

"Probably not. The place I have in mind is ten minutes out. There's a diner and a gas station, that's it."

"Well, that's just crazy," she muttered. "How can any-place not have decent internet in this day and age? Have people not heard of satellites?"

Trent grinned. "You're not in Kansas anymore, darlin'."

She raised her brows at him. "Darlin'?"

"At least I didn't call you sweetheart."

She let out a disgusted sigh. But he saw the small smile before she looked down at her phone. He thought she'd found a local cell tower, but she didn't call until they'd parked in front of the roadside diner. Instead of heading in, she told him she'd be along in a minute and wandered off to a private spot.

So she didn't want him to hear her conversation. Fine. As he'd told himself a hundred times, none of his business.

Let her have her secrets.

After all, Trent had one hell of a doozy of his own.

# 10

As the truck bounced along the rough, pitted road Shelby stared at the ranch they were approaching. It looked like a small village. There were far more buildings than she could account for with her limited knowledge of ranching.

She was about to ask Trent what they were all for when he turned onto a paved driveway and drove under the elaborate wrought-iron archway announcing the Castle Ranch. Elm trees turning gold and red lined the seemingly endless driveway. The terrain was hillier than at the Eager Beaver and well-maintained.

"Wow, it's pretty out here." She twisted around to watch a pair of beautiful white horses galloping, the epitome of grace and beauty. "Is this all one ranch?"

"Yep."

She saw the main house. Who could miss the gorgeous, sprawling Tudor-style home with all the natural stone and glass? The sloping manicured lawn that surrounded it was impossibly green.

On the far right stood a long white structure that had to be the bunkhouse. Two men standing in front talking turned and lifted their hands in friendly waves, which Shelby returned.

The large rust-colored barns were easy to identify, all three of them. A few other scattered buildings were probably sheds, although five times the size by her definition.

"I think you're wrong about this being all one ranch," she said, pointing to a cluster of four small houses each with its own yard and beds of faded flowers.

Trent glanced at them with a faint smile. "The married hired hands live in those."

"Are you serious?" She stared at him, then got distracted by their surroundings again. "They have their own gas station?"

He laughed. "A place this size runs a lot of equipment. Those two gas pumps are more necessity than convenience."

"Huh." Closer to the house was an impressive building in both size and appearance. "What's that?"

"The stable," he said, frowning at her as if she'd committed blasphemy by needing to ask.

"Right." She noticed what had to be a racetrack but refrained from commenting.

A tall distinguished-looking man with white hair walked out of the stable and motioned for Trent to park under a large cottonwood tree.

Trent eased the truck into the spot and cut the engine. "Is this how you expected the Eager Beaver to look?"

"Oh, sure." She scanned the front of the house. The stone work was awesome, and so was the aggregate circular drive sweeping around hundreds of yellow mums. The whole place was really something. "I didn't even know ranches like this existed outside of the movies."

"You should see some of the spreads in Texas." He grabbed his black Stetson from the backseat and put it on. "Ready?"

She nodded. "Don't worry. I won't ask any more stupid questions."

"Ask anything you want," he said, grinning as he got out of the truck.

She did a quick check in the visor mirror. She'd gotten rid of the scarf, mittens and her coat before going into the diner but her hair was still flat so she poufed it out some.

Her door opened. Trent stood there holding it for her. "You look great," he said with a trace of amusement.

Accepting the hand he offered, she slid off the seat and touched ground. "So do you," she said and winked.

His low sexy chuckle did a number on her nervous system. As if being confined to the truck's cab for two hours, sitting close enough to notice the spot he'd missed shaving and admiring his firm, chiseled jaw hadn't already left her a tad weak in the knees.

They headed toward the man who stood outside the stable, cleaning his sunglasses while waiting for them. He wore perfectly creased black jeans and a crisp long-sleeve blue shirt. Shelby didn't really know boots but she'd be willing to bet his cost as much as her entire shoe collection, which was nothing to sneeze at.

"Mr. Calhoun." Trent approached with his hand extended.

"Trent Kimball." The man folded his white handkerchief slowly and slipped it into his pocket, then put on his aviator-style sunglasses, adjusting them carefully. Finally, he shook Trent's hand. "Call me Hank. We're all friends here." He smiled at Shelby. "And who's this?"

"Shel—"

"Shelby Foster," she said, not meaning to cut Trent off, and automatically offered Mr. Calhoun her hand.

"A pleasure to make your acquaintance." He picked up her hand and kissed the back.

Startled, she pressed her lips together and forced a smile. He was older, from a different generation, and was just being polite…

Like hell. While working for the Williamsons, she'd dealt with a wide range of wealthy clients, up to and including the obscenely rich. She'd found most of them to be pleasant and reasonable. But there had been a few, rude, arrogant men like Hank Calhoun. Though she'd never before experienced such a strong and instant dislike for someone.

Maybe she'd rushed to judgment. But she doubted it. His posturing was too obvious. First, he'd made no move to greet Trent, then left him standing with his hand out while the jerk wiped his glasses?

And then kissing her hand? Calhoun knew better. All she'd offered was a handshake.

Ew. Now she needed a shower.

But this was Trent's show so she kept a smile in place, calmly withdrew her hand.

"Quite a spread you have here," Trent said, glancing around. "You raise cattle, too, don't you?"

Glad for the change of subject, she breathed out a sigh of relief that neither man appeared to have noticed her reaction.

"My sons handle that side of the business," Calhoun said with a dismissive wave. "I have a much greater interest in horses. Arabians in particular."

Trent gave him an odd look, frowned for a moment, then said, "Mind showing me inside your stable?" His gaze followed the high pitch of the roof. "I'm already green with envy."

Calhoun laughed. "Sure, I'll give you a tour. A little later, though." Trent didn't seem pleased. "Have you folks eaten yet? I have a terrific cook. Ruth will whip up anything you want."

"No, thanks." Trent patted his flat belly, drawing Shelby's attention. "We stopped on the way."

Her gaze lingered on his narrow waist and hips. Today

he wore a blue chambray shirt tucked into his jeans. They weren't very worn but still fit him nice and snug.

"Shelby?" Trent touched her arm.

She blinked.

Both men were looking at her.

Her mind had been wiped clean. She couldn't come up with a blessed thing to say.

"Would you like something to drink?" Trent asked, a gleam of amusement in his gray eyes.

"I'm good. Thanks. Would you excuse me a moment?" She took a step back. "Don't wait. I'll catch up," she said, then turned and walked to the truck as quickly as she could manage without tripping, keeping her head down and taking deep breaths.

She'd been staring at Trent's fly.

Of course he'd noticed. And in case he'd chalked it up to his imagination, she'd just provided confirmation by stalking off like a two-year-old. Her cheeks had to be flaming every shade of red.

She climbed into the truck and slid down in the seat. There had to be good internet here. She couldn't see Hank Calhoun tolerating spotty service. Reaching for her coat, which was on the backseat, she pulled her cell from the pocket. A quick glance assured her the men had continued their discussion and showed no interest in her. She focused on her cell. Busy morning. Texts from Donald and the movers. A voice mail from her mom. And one from Mrs. Williamson, Donald's mother. That was a first. And it presented a tricky problem. The woman had been Shelby's employer for five years. It could be a business call.

After all, Shelby had left without much notice, something that would haunt her conscience for a long time. Although she had tried to tough out a week, just to tie up loose ends if nothing else. But Donald had refused to leave her alone. And if Mrs. Williamson could've killed her with a look, Shelby would be dead by now. The hostile work environment hadn't inspired creativity so instead of finishing the week Shelby had left the next day.

She scrolled through texts—the movers needed to hear from her ASAP. So did Donald. She felt badly about not setting up a delivery appointment last night so she called the movers before listening to messages. And was sent straight to voice mail. Okay with her since she was still iffy about what to tell them.

Bracing herself for Mrs. Williamson's message, Shelby hit Speaker and let her gaze wander toward Trent and Hank standing at the fence surrounding the racetrack. The men were too far away to make out Trent's expression. But she recognized his body language. Arms folded, shoulders back, jaw angled up. He looked pissed.

Hank gestured with his hands, clearly talking about the horse and rider running around the track. She would've never guessed he could be so animated.

Her cell beeped signaling the end of the voice mail. She hadn't heard a word of it. Quickly she replayed the message while opening the truck door. Mrs. Williamson's sickeningly sweet tone was a complete surprise, and enough to make Shelby nauseous. The woman usually reserved the syrupy voice for rich clients. Shelby listened a bit, then disconnected. Pleading on behalf of her grown son…for God's sake. But then the overbearing woman had become a big part of the problem between Shelby and Donald. Everything had to be his mother's way, and Donald didn't seem to care. He just took the easy path to keep the peace. But so had Shelby. Until she'd realized Donald would never be on her side. He'd never appreciate her need to be her own person. His mother would always rule.

Because Shelby didn't want to be rude, she would eventually return Mrs. Williamson's call. But for now she slipped the phone into her jeans pocket, more interested in Trent and whether he needed reinforcements. As she got closer, she saw Hank hold up a stopwatch just as the horse, the rider crouched forward in jockey position, ran past them.

"Look at that." He motioned to someone inside the fence. The young man was bent forward, hands on his thighs, squinting at the horse's legs, but he waved an acknowledgement. "Tell me that isn't a damn fine-looking animal," Hank said and clapped Trent on the back.

"No argument from me," Trent said, unsmiling.

"People have underestimated Arabians. The racing world started to wake up in the nineties, but the breed still has too few tracks available to them. But you wait. In the next five years, these beauties will win higher purses than any quarter horse could dream of."

Shelby stood on Trent's left, not sure if he'd seen her yet. She brushed her arm against his.

He turned and gave her a smile. "Everything okay?" he asked quietly.

"Service is great here," she said, holding up the phone. "So yay."

Hank glanced at her, then swung his attention back to the track. "You'll appreciate this next stallion. I bought Thor a few months ago. He's four years old and he's already won his first race. With the right trainer, I think he could be a real money maker. I got him for a steal. The idiots who owned him had no idea what they were doing."

Shelby reminded herself that horseracing, ranching and horse trading, or whatever they called it, were businesses. A difficult concept to grasp when the commodity was a gorgeous gray horse with an impressive mane that looked like silk. But obviously Hank had brokered a good deal. She shouldn't dislike him more than she already did because of it. Yet she did.

The silver-gray stallion pranced onto the track as if the

whole world were watching. He flicked his tail, arched his neck slightly. With his gleaming coat, Thor was really that breathtaking.

"He's beautiful," she whispered, unable to tear her gaze away. "Isn't he?"

Trent heaved a sigh.

She felt his breath on her face. Felt the heat from his body, startled to discover that she was leaning into him. And with a fair amount of her weight. She immediately straightened.

He slid an arm around her and lightly squeezed her left shoulder. "Yes, he is."

"What was that?" Hank asked her, then proved he'd heard by adding, "The lady has excellent taste. Watch him, Kimball. You'll be impressed."

Trent kept his eyes on the horse, his hand on her shoulder. She could still feel his tension and wished she understood what was wrong.

For the next twenty minutes they watched Thor beat his last recorded time. Then Hank showed them another horse, a bay mare, who apparently needed a lot of training. Hank continued to communicate with hand signals, though sometimes using his cell to give curt orders to the men running the horses. The whole time Trent remained silent.

Finally, he spoke. "You have a nice setup here, Hank. Some impressive horses. Glad I got to see it. But at this point, there's no sense wasting any more of each other's time."

As he turned to Trent, the other man's mouth tightened. "You don't want the job?"

"Like I told you, I don't work with Thoroughbreds or Arabians. I've got nothing against them. But I only train quarter horses."

Hank removed his sunglasses and narrowed his dark

eyes. "I know for a fact you trained a winning Thorough-bred for Tucker Lawson."

"Hell, that was over seven years ago, and I only did it as a favor."

Hank studied him with a critical eye. "After what happened in Texas, I figured you wouldn't be so picky."

Trent stared at the man until Hank looked away. "Guess you thought wrong."

"Is it the money?" Hank asked, taking a hundred-and-eighty degree swing with a kiss-ass tone that seemed to irritate Trent even more. "Look, whatever they were paying you in Texas, I'll double."

"Nice meeting you, Mr. Calhoun. I wish you well." Trent extended his hand.

Hank ignored it. "All right," he said, sounding petulant again. "You can take Thor and Aces to your place. I've never allowed any of my horses to be trained anywhere but Castle Ranch. This is a damn big concession for me."

"I'm sure another trainer will appreciate it." Trent shook his head. "Look, I'm not trying to play hard to get or squeeze you for more money." He shrugged. "I'm really not interested."

"I'll go six-figures as well as winning bonus," Calhoun said with a smug lift of his chin. "How's that?"

Trent didn't even blink. He turned, gave her a tired smile and steered them toward the truck.

"No one else will offer you a better deal," Calhoun called out, then added something completely undignified.

"Someone needs to tell him he's too old to be a sore loser," Shelby muttered.

Trent stopped on the passenger side and opened the door for her. "Think I'm a fool for turning down all that money?"

"No." She looked up at him. "I think you'd be nuts to

work for an egomaniac who has more money than brains.
For God's sake, he didn't have enough sense to be tactful."

He waited until she'd slid onto the seat. And then he
leaned in and kissed her.

His lips were warm and firm, patient. She had a feeling
he'd intended to keep it light. But when she strained up to
meet him partway, he became more insistent, the increasing pressure of his mouth matching her eager reaction. At
the first touch of his tongue she parted her lips.

He slid inside, then cupped her jaw with his slightly
calloused hand while his tongue made a thorough sweep.
Good thing she was already sitting down. It was as if he'd
found a magic switch. Her whole body jolted to life. She
put a hand on his arm and the swell of his bicep under her
palm sent a tingling sensation skipping down her spine.

Trent pulled back, his breathing ragged. "Let's get out
of here before Calhoun turns a hose on us."

She laughed, stopped abruptly. "God, he probably would
do something like that, wouldn't he?" When she saw Trent
staring at her mouth and making no move to plant himself
behind the wheel, she said, "Well, get in already."

"Yes, ma'am," he said, and stole another quick kiss before climbing into the truck.

TRENT'S CARELESS DISREGARD for his promise to stay away
from Shelby hit him hard. So did Shelby's reaction. The
kiss had been a give and take, and, damn it, he wanted
more. He seriously considered pulling the truck to the
side of the road to finish what he'd started back at Castle
Ranch. So much for being noble.

Even now, when he was focused on driving, the taste of
her was still strong in his mouth. The feel of her soft skin
still plagued his memory. He didn't know if he could trust
his own word. Telling himself to stay away from her and

believing he could do it had been a whole lot easier when she wasn't within reach.

"Are you having second thoughts?" she asked, breaking the tension-filled silence.

"About?"

"Calhoun's offer."

He shook his head. "I'd never work for someone so controlling. Hell, I've trained Thoroughbreds and Arabians, and I'd do it again. They're good horses. But he'd led me to believe he had quarter horses which he obviously doesn't, and that pissed me off."

"I'm glad you won't work for him. Not that you need my approval."

He thought about his ex-wife and how she would've been fawning all over the man. As Trent had eventually discovered, a guy's net worth was what impressed Dana. Power came a close second. Everything had been just fine between them when he'd been pulling in big bonuses. She would've called him three kinds of stupid for turning down Calhoun's money.

Shelby wasn't like that. But then he barely knew her. He and Dana had been married for a couple of years before he'd seen that side of her. Maybe he just hadn't been paying attention.

Anyway, he had no business comparing the two women. Man, he used to hate it when his dad had compared him to his older brother.

Naturally, Trent always ended up with the short end of the stick. Colby was nearly a carbon copy of their dad. Though he tended to stay with a job or project a good while longer. But ultimately, when things got rough, he'd quit just like their old man and move on to something else.

Trent was the exact opposite, and while he hadn't actually been called an overachiever, he knew that's what his dad believed. Maybe Trent's successes made him feel uncomfortable with his own failures.

He glanced at Shelby and caught her watching him. Probably curious about what had happened in Texas, but she didn't ask. She smiled before looking away.

"I have another quick stop to have a look at that colt. It'll take forty minutes, tops. After that, we'll head to Blackfoot Falls and see about getting you a fair booth. You still game?"

Her eyes flashed with excitement. "Totally."

Three months.

Hell, he'd never make it.

# *11*

SINCE THE MAYOR'S office was closed, they tried Abe's Variety next. Posters were up all over town about the fair. It seemed to be a bigger deal than Trent remembered. He'd last been to the fair when he'd visited Colby and his family, the year before his brother had given up on the Eager Beaver.

After the usual few minutes of jawing about nothing, Abe sent them to the Watering Hole. According to him, Sadie, the owner of the bar, had been helping the mayor's secretary with organizing this year's event. Made for some interesting speculation since Sadie was running for mayor in the November election, against Clarence Leland who'd remained in office, unopposed, for twelve years.

Trent imagined the situation gave everyone a lot to talk about. In fact, showing up with Shelby was likely to add a lot more spice to the gossip stew. Some things just never changed no matter how many years he'd been away.

Sadie had opened for business five minutes earlier, and she stood with her hands on her hips, facing the door when they walked into the bar.

Trent laughed. Shelby stared up at him with a puzzled frown. He knew right away Abe had already called

Sadie with a heads-up, and Shelby would understand soon enough.

"The fair is next weekend," Sadie said. "Three weeks later than usual because Mayor Leland, in all his finite wisdom—as in thimble-size—decided we should team up with Cooper County this year. And now you think you can waltz your sweet-talking self in here and flatter me into renting you a booth this late in the game?"

"Yep." Trent grinned. "In a nutshell."

"Well, you're right." Sadie laughed, then swatted him away when he tried to kiss her cheek. She went behind the bar and pulled out a form from a manila folder wedged in next to the cash register. "Fill this out and give me forty bucks."

Trent automatically reached into his pocket at the same time Shelby opened her purse.

"Now, this should be interesting." Sadie leaned forward, resting her forearms on the bar, her face full of mischief and amusement.

He caught Shelby's warning look and lifted both hands in surrender. "Just a reflex." He glanced at Sadie. "This is Shelby."

The older woman nodded. "We met the other day at Abe's store."

"Just forty dollars…really?" Shelby glanced at the form as she passed her the money. "The county must get a percentage of sales, then."

"Nope. We try to keep it simple. We don't have many outside vendors come in. Mostly it's local folks and we like giving them the chance to make a little extra money."

Shelby looked disappointed.

"What are you planning on selling?" Sadie asked.

"Jewelry. Nothing very expensive. I make the pieces myself."

"You should do okay," Sadie said. "No one else will

have jewelry for sale. And Christmas will be here before you know it."

"She'll do better than okay," Trent said, completely convinced. "Wait till you see her jewelry. It's really something."

Sadie gave him a soft, knowing smile. Shelby was staring at him with a wary expression. What had he said that justified that look? He was just being honest.

Behind him the door opened. A young cowboy Trent didn't recognize stuck his head inside as if looking for someone.

Sadie straightened. "You'll have to fill the form out right now and not mention this to anyone," she said in a hushed voice. "You missed the deadline by two weeks."

"I don't want you getting in trouble over this."

"Nah, she won't. Sadie's gonna be our next mayor," Trent said and grinned at her snort of disgust.

"I'll tell you what…" Sadie slid a pen across the bar to Shelby. "The idea of giving that old blowhard a run for his money was a whole lot more appealing than actually running against him. Sometimes I think that man hasn't got the brains of a grasshopper."

Trent didn't know the guy, and while he'd always liked Sadie, he couldn't picture her as mayor. But then he'd lived most of his adult life close to Dallas and maybe in a place the size of Blackfoot Falls, Sadie was just the person the town needed.

"I didn't even ask…you two want anything to drink?"

Shelby looked up from the form. "A cola would be great, or anything with caffeine."

Sadie smiled, nodded. "Trent?"

"Much as I'd like a beer, I'll take a soda. We have to hit the road as soon as Shelby finishes. I've got a colt waiting in the trailer."

"You just buy him?"

Nodding, he dug into his pocket. "From the Landers over at the Whispering Pines."

"Good people. I heard they have top-notch stock." Sadie set the colas in front of them. "I haven't seen Violet for a while. How's the old girl doing?"

"Ornery as ever," Trent said, and saw a smile twitch at the corners of Shelby's mouth as she kept writing.

"Tell you the truth, I'm glad you're back and not paying attention to that silly curse," Sadie said. "Violet shouldn't be living out there alone."

Shelby's head came up, her gaze narrowed. "What curse?"

"I'm pretty sure I mentioned it to you," Trent said and took a sip to hide his amusement.

"But I knew you were trying to get rid of me so I didn't believe you."

Chuckling, Sadie traded glances between the two of them. "Don't worry, honey. It's nothing but nonsense anyway."

"I'd still like to hear it."

Sadie shrugged. "It goes back a few generations. Has something to do with anyone trying to make a go of the Eager Beaver being doomed to fail. Don't know who started it. Do you, Trent?"

"I heard it might've been my great-granddad." Trent glanced at Shelby. It only now occurred to him that it could've been her great-grandfather since he'd left angry. But he wasn't about to say anything.

"Of course your pa had horrible luck trying to make a living off the place. And so did your brother, bless his heart." Sadie shook her head. "I'm not saying there's anything to the curse, mind you…"

Trent drained his cola. The subject was closed as far as he was concerned. He couldn't afford to think he might be the next Kimball who failed. "You about finished?" he asked Shelby. "Time to get on the road."

She looked blankly at him, before giving him an absent nod. After checking two more boxes on the form, she passed the paper and pen to Sadie. "Thanks so much for letting me have the booth. I promise not to tell a soul," she said as she slid off the stool.

Sadie snorted a laugh. "Well, you'll never fit in around here."

Although Shelby smiled, something was obviously bothering her.

Sadie stuck the form in the manila folder, then turned back to see Trent pulling money out of his pocket. "Oh, for pity's sake, all you had were colas. Put that away."

"No, ma'am, we can't have it appear that you're bribing voters." Smiling at her eye-roll, he slid a ten-dollar bill under his glass and noticed Shelby had left something, too. Which was unnecessary but none of his business. "Good luck with the campaigning."

"Thank you again," Shelby said, following him to the door.

He held it open for her, wondering what had her worrying her lower lip and looking plain ol' depressed.

Two cowboys who'd been about to enter the bar stepped aside for them. The taller man tipped his Stetson at Shelby. Both of them stared like idiots. She favored them with a polite smile as she passed, then continued down the sidewalk oblivious to their fascination with her backside.

Trent almost said something. But that would be dumb. Not only did he have no right, but how many times had he done the same thing, himself? Shelby hadn't seen them anyway, so why make matters worse? He did the next best thing and walked directly behind her, cutting off their view.

A minute later she stopped and looked from side to side, before spinning around to face him. "Where were you?"

"Right here." He dug out his keys. "Look, if you'd like

to hang around town for a while, I could take the colt and trailer back to the Eager Beaver and pick you up later."

She'd already started shaking her head before he finished. "Thanks, but I have a lot of work to do for the fair." Her smile was for him alone. "If you don't mind, I'd really like to go home."

He didn't miss the slight catch in her voice at the end. He also didn't miss that he might have already crossed from none of his business to very much his concern.

AFTER TAKING A short walk with Mutt, Shelby stopped at the equipment shed for a peek inside. It was definitely roomier than she'd imagined and cleaner, with a raised wood plank floor to keep the contents dry.

On the drive to Castle Ranch two days earlier, Trent had assured her there was adequate space for her belongings. She missed sleeping in her own bed, which she decided would go into her room along with the cherry nightstand and matching dresser. It would be crowded but she didn't mind. Living out of a suitcase was starting to get to her.

"I heard you got movers coming tomorrow."

Startled by Violet's voice, Shelby jerked back and banged her head on the doorframe.

"Ouch." The woman's rusty cackle turned into a brief cough. "Thought you might've heard me come up behind you."

Shelby made sure she'd cleared the doorway before turning around. And caught a nasty whiff of Violet's pipe. Her cough sounded worrisome, yet she was still puffing away.

"The delivery truck should arrive midmorning," Shelby said and rubbed the side of her head. "I don't have much so they shouldn't be here long, but I'll make sure they don't block the driveway."

"Hell, they could be here all day. Won't make no difference to me." Violet moved closer to the shed for a better look inside. "You storing your things out here?" she asked, frowning.

"Some of them… Trent offered the third bedroom."

"Did he now?" Violet looked oddly pleased.

"Yes, he's been very accommodating. He even helped me get a booth at the fair so I can sell my jewelry."

Violet eyed Shelby's ragged jeans and disgraceful fingernails. "You make the baubles yourself?"

"I do." She plucked at her faded pink T-shirt. "I've been working a lot trying to increase my inventory."

Mutt returned from chasing one thing or another. Sniffing Violet's pocket, he stared up at her with hopeful eyes and a wagging tail.

"Always looking for a handout, ain't you?" There was no hiding her fondness for the dog. She dug deep in the oversize coveralls and gave him a giant Milk-Bone. "Now git."

Shelby laughed.

"The dog's a pain in the neck just like his master," Violet grumbled.

"Uh-huh. You know I don't buy this act, right? You adore both of them."

"Baloney. Wait till you've been here awhile—"

Shelby sighed. Awhile meant three months tops for her, and if she was any kind of decent human being she wouldn't put Trent through the inconvenience of an unwanted guest for that long.

"What was that sigh for?"

"I should put my things in storage. Trent is being great, and I'm being horrible and selfish. I know I don't have a claim here." Shelby massaged her left temple. "We all know it."

Violet removed the pipe from her mouth and slanted a glance toward the house. "He inside?"

"I think so."

The woman's troubled frown rested on Shelby. "I need to get something off my chest. But before I do, you've got to swear you won't repeat it." Violet paused, her solemn expression making Shelby wary. "I mean it. I want you to swear on your great-granddaddy's grave."

Shelby tensed. What if the woman was ill? What if keeping her secret meant life or death? What if—

"Well, all right," Violet said with a resigned nod. "I respect a person who won't give their word too freely."

"Wait." Shelby couldn't just let her walk away. Violet clearly needed an ear. "You can talk to me. And I promise whatever it is stays between us."

"You sure? It'll be mighty tempting to run straight to Trent."

Now Shelby was just plain curious. "I'm sure."

Violet's eyes bore into hers. "It's about the Eager Beaver. I believe the ranch belongs to you, Shelby Foster. And in ten days I'll be able to prove it."

SHELBY SHOULD'VE BEEN doing a jig. Or grinning from ear to ear. At the very least, she should feel relieved knowing she would have a roof over her head for as long as she wanted to stay in Blackfoot Falls.

Still shocked by what Violet had confided, Shelby entered the house through the front door and glanced around. The leather recliner and couch, the dark wood coffee table, the large widescreen TV pretty much summed up the living room. And left little doubt a man lived here. Even thinking about where to put her own furniture felt wrong.

Maybe Violet was mistaken. Four generations of Kimballs had lived here, a fact verified by several unbiased townspeople. How weird was it that Shelby almost hoped Violet had gotten confused.

Another thing that didn't add up was the woman's lack

of concern for Trent. Those two shared a fondness for each other, and no argument could convince Shelby otherwise. Violet wouldn't want to see him lose out. Maybe she simply expected Shelby to do the right thing, whatever that was.

She heard a low murmur coming from the kitchen. Trent was probably watching a YouTube video on his laptop. He did that a lot when he wasn't working outside. Mostly, though, he kept the computer in his room where she wouldn't walk in and surprise him.

She was fairly certain it was the same video that he'd watched over and over again, and she thought she understood what compelled him to do so.

It was about what had happened in Texas. He hadn't told her about the fateful race. And she hadn't asked. But she knew because she'd looked him up online when they'd come back with the colt. She wasn't proud of being nosy and intrusive, but ever since the meeting with Hank Calhoun, Trent hadn't been quite himself.

Entering the kitchen, she saw him sitting at the table, hunched forward, his attention glued to the computer screen. She made a noise to alert him to her presence. He surprised her by not closing the laptop as he'd always done. After a quick glance at her, he extended his arms over his head and arched back into a serious stretch.

"Man, that feels good," he murmured, his eyes drifting closed.

She let her gaze follow the ridge of muscles defining his arm, trailing the width of his broad shoulders and straining his T-shirt. A flash of memory of him working shirtless provided details of his bare chest and belly. She stopped in the middle of the kitchen, her insides fluttering as though a whole flock of hummingbirds was trying to escape.

Her feet wouldn't move. All she could do was stare. The thick dark lashes, the day's growth of beard covering his chin and jaw, the attractive shape of his lips. She remembered the feel of them against her mouth, as if they'd kissed only minutes ago.

Midway through a long contented moan, he opened his eyes.

She simply stood there, offering a sheepish smile. And doing everything within her power to not make matters worse by looking at the laptop.

"I was about to put water on for tea. Would you like some?" Oh, brother, she knew he didn't drink tea. "Or anything else while I'm up?"

The faint smile he hid made her cheeks warm. But he pulled his arms in and straightened in his seat, his eyes dark and speculative, never leaving her face. "When you're finished, I'd like to show you something."

"Sure." She hurriedly stuck a mug of water in the microwave, set it to heat for two minutes, and brought out an herbal tea bag. "Okay," she said and joined him at the table.

Trent looked her directly in the eyes and asked, "Did anyone tell you about what happened in Texas?"

"No." It was the truth. Also a technicality, because she knew what he was getting at. In spite of herself, she blinked. "But I think I know."

He rubbed his jaw, sighing at the laptop now in screen-saver mode. "Damn YouTube."

"And Wiki."

Turning back to her, he snorted a laugh. "You did a search?"

She opened her mouth to deny it, then just pressed her lips together and nodded. "For what it's worth, I read very little."

His wry expression made her wish she'd kept her mouth shut. "I don't know what you found," he said, shrugging. "Basically, I tried to pull a horse from a race. He had a badly bruised sole. I was afraid it might abscess. The vet had given him a non-steroidal anti-inflammatory. But he shouldn't have run. The owner and I had a heated discussion, which unfortunately was overheard. He disagreed with me, let Race the Moon run. Moon placed...that means came in second. I made a wrong call that could've cost the owner forty thousand dollars."

"So he fired you."

"No." Trent touched the screen, bringing it back to life. "I left before the race started."

"Because you knew he would fire you later?" she asked, studying his carefully blank expression. "Or was it because you no longer trusted him?"

He turned away from the screen and met her eyes. "I know for a fact you didn't read that anywhere."

Shaking her head, Shelby smiled. "I think you still believe you made the right call."

His gaze narrowed. "Because?"

"How many times have you watched the video?" She nodded at the laptop. "I doubt it's to punish yourself."

Trent raised his brows. "The thing is, I don't want to think Paul would do anything underhanded or risk injuring a horse. But I really believe he gave Moon an injection to block the nerves...it's for pain. And illegal as far as racing goes."

"How long had you worked for him?"

"Six years." His shrug didn't fool her. A hint of sadness had crept into his voice.

"I'm sorry to say I know nothing about horseracing." She gestured to the laptop. "But may I?"

"Sure." He angled it so she could see the screen just as the microwave dinged. Instead of getting up, she scooted her chair closer to his. "Get your tea," he said. "I'll wait."

"Later." She leaned closer so they could both see, hoping he'd explain what was happening in the video. Her left leg pressed against his right. Their shoulders touched.

The temperature in the kitchen seemed to rise considerably.

Her face and chest felt warm as she tried to get comfortable without doing more touching. She kept her eyes on the screen.

He started the video, then all he said was, "Number 11."

She spotted the chestnut-colored horse right after he left the gate. He was a beauty, shiny and sleek with muscle. She watched him break from the pack along with two other horses. A minute later Race the Moon crossed the finish line a nose behind a gray stallion.

Shelby turned to Trent. "Will you ever know if you made the right call?"

"No. I can't know for sure. You saw it yourself, Moon looked great," he said, shrugging. "A month later he was supposed to run again, but he was scratched at the last minute. After that, there's been nothing. I hope he isn't hurt permanently. I admit, I started watching the video again after he was pulled, hoping to see something that would show me the truth."

"So if he couldn't run that second time, doesn't that mean you were probably right?"

Trent smiled. "Maybe. That doesn't help Moon."

"Can I ask you something?"

"Go ahead."

"What if it had gone the other way? If you'd thought Moon shouldn't race, and you'd kept quiet for whatever reason, and Moon was hurt…could you have lived with yourself?"

He frowned at her as if she'd just asked the stupidest question on earth.

"I'll take that as a no," she said when silence stretched. "That means you made the right call." She scooted her chair back. "You were trying to protect Moon. Personally, I'm glad you're that man."

Trent blinked.

She got to her feet. The water for her tea would be cold by now. She turned to the microwave but stopped when he caught her hand. Startled, she heard his chair scrape back, then he was on his feet, tugging her around to face him.

He released her hand and stared into her eyes. A slow smile curved his mouth as he touched her cheek. His finger trailed to her chin, nudging it up as he lowered his head.

# 12

THEIR LIPS MET in a warm, soft kiss. A hand cupped the left side of Shelby's waist. Resting her palm on his chest, she lifted herself onto her tiptoes. As the kiss deepened her heart beat faster.

Trent put both arms around her and re-angled his head. The second she parted her lips he slipped his tongue between them and slowly explored the inside of her mouth. She hadn't seen this coming, and she doubted he had, either. Not that she objected.

She slid her hand up to his shoulder, pausing to savor the feel of hard muscles bunching under her palm. He deepened the kiss, his arms tightening around her until she rubbed up against something else that was hard and thrilling.

"Jesus." He moaned quietly against her tongue. On a deep breath, he broke the kiss and, with his head tipped back, briefly closed his eyes. When they finally met hers once more, they were dark with desire and sexy as hell. "This is all wrong," he said.

Regret erased everything in a single heartbeat. Shelby swallowed, confused, and not sure what to do. They were still touching. Her hand stayed frozen on his shoulder, and he'd only loosened his arms but hadn't let go. She moistened her lips. "Why?"

His brows drew together in a slight frown. Once she noticed that his bottom lip was damp, she couldn't seem to drag her gaze away. That kiss wasn't wrong. Not to her.

"Shelby?"

"What?"

He let go then, and she looked up.

"I know you're hurting," he said, his voice low and careful. "I won't take advantage of you like this."

Even more confused, she stepped back, letting her own hand fall away. "Hurting?"

"Fresh off a broken engagement? It's rough. I know."

"Oh." Her sigh ended with a laugh. "Do I sound like a stone-cold bitch admitting I feel the best I have in three years?" She wrinkled her nose. "No, probably more like four."

Trent looked as though he wanted to believe her but couldn't quite get there.

She probably should feel guilty. And occasionally she did, but only because in her heart she'd known for a while that being with Donald meant giving up too much of herself.

"I do." She shrugged. "If anything, I'm embarrassed for taking so long to man up, so to speak. I stayed too long because I was a big chicken. But that's history. I really appreciate it, though. That you cared enough to stop."

A blush heated her cheeks, and she made herself walk very calmly to get her tea.

"What you said earlier, about how things turned out with Moon…and…"

She'd only made it a few steps before turning back to him.

"…and how you're glad I'm that man." The intensity

of his gaze made her toes curl. "I want you to know I appreciate it."

*Screw the tea.* She moved closer. "Is that why you kissed me?"

Letting out a short laugh, he rubbed his jaw. "Might've started out that way."

"And…" She returned her hand to his shoulder and watched a lazy, arrogant smile tug at his mouth.

"You asking for trouble, darlin'?"

"Really?" She stepped back, narrowing her eyes. "So you don't want me in your bed?" she asked sweetly, darting away when he reached for her.

"Wait." He caught her around the waist and lifted her off the floor until they were eye to eye. "I'll swear on a stack of Bibles never to call you that again."

"Don't bother," she said, leaning in for the quickest of kisses. "We'll just find a notary pub—" She let out a squeak when he lifted her higher and nipped at the stiff nipple straining against her shirt. Heat swept her body. She dug her fingers into his shoulder muscles. "Can Violet see in here?"

His gaze shot to the window. "Depends. How about we—"

"Yes." She expected him to set her down. "Hey, I can walk."

Trent just laughed. "I know. I've admired the view many times."

Still in no apparent hurry to let her feet touch the linoleum, he kissed her jaw, then her chin, holding her in the air as if she weighed no more than a marshmallow. He let her down a couple more inches and brushed his lips across hers.

She felt the hardness behind the fly of his jeans and knew he wouldn't last long. In truth, she doubted she would, either.

All it took was a little strategic squirming, and he set her down. Taking her by the hand, he led her quickly through the living room and straight to his bedroom.

It was a decent size with a king sleigh bed, matching dresser and a single nightstand. Everything was very neat. The bed wasn't completely made but a dark blue quilt had been pulled to the top, smoothed out and partly tucked.

"Bigger bed," was all he said before he tugged up the hem of her faded T-shirt. Too late she remembered what he'd find underneath.

Damn, why couldn't she be wearing one of her pretty lace bras?

"Uh, this doesn't actually work unless you lift up your arms."

"I don't want to," she whined.

He gave her a long look, then laughed. It was cut short when she unbuckled his belt and went for his jeans.

"Hold on." He stopped her, raked a worried gaze down her shirt. "You're really not going to let me take that off?"

She thought of telling him to wait and rushing to her room to change, but… "I'm wearing a sports bra."

"Okay."

"Because I was working…and, well, it's more comfortable…" She sighed. Trent clearly had no idea what she meant. He gave her that slow sexy smile of his, and thumbed her sensitive nipple through the worn material.

Shelby sucked in a breath. "Fine," she said, and pulled the ratty T-shirt off.

He stared at the industrial-strength sports bra. Frowning, he leaned over for a quick glance at the back. "I have no idea what to do with this."

At his adorably bewildered expression, she burst out laughing. "Undress yourself, I'll take care of it."

She didn't have to tell him twice.

He went right to work, yanking off his T-shirt, pulling

off his boots and jeans. All that was left were his boxer-briefs when he stopped to stare at her.

Thank goodness for the tiny bikini panties. The way he was looking at them, she kind of hated to take them off. Although his interest shifted the second he noticed her bra was gone. With laser focus he stared at her bare breasts.

His mouth curved in a half smile, he moved closer. "Okay, now I know what I'm doing." He touched a nipple with his finger, then bent and rolled his tongue over it.

At the slight rasp of stubble against her skin, Shelby shivered. She plunged her hands into his dark wavy hair. His musky, thoroughly masculine scent teased her nostrils. He dropped to a crouch and kissed a spot between her ribs while slipping off her panties.

Once he got them off, he reached around and squeezed her butt, pulling her against his mouth, trailing his lips lower, to her belly, then lingering just above the V of her thighs.

The intimate feel of his warm breath sent heat racing through her body. Swaying slightly, she moved her hands from his hair to clutch his shoulders. She'd felt dizzy for a moment. Probably the lack of air in her lungs. One second she'd been inhaling his scent, the next she'd forgotten how to breathe altogether.

After pressing a final kiss to her tingling skin, he rose. "You okay?"

"Yes, except..." She hooked a finger in his waistband. "You still have clothes on."

With a choked laugh, he got down to nothing but a cocky grin and an impressive hard-on. She looked her fill as he yanked back the covers, and got all tingly when he kept looking back at her. He came around the bed, put his hands on her waist and pulled her against him.

His kiss was hot and thorough and scrambled her senses. He was much taller than her now that her feet were bare. As his mouth grew more demanding, her head went back and he moved a hand to cradle her skull as he gentled the kiss.

She pushed her palms up his chest, tunneled her fingers into his hair, and sighed when he wrapped his arms around her and held her tight. He was all hard muscle and smooth skin. His arousal felt hot and insistent pressed to her belly and she couldn't wait. After more kissing, he guided her the few steps to the bed and laid her down, so gently it surprised her.

Not that she'd expected him to be rough or clumsy. She just had never been with a rugged sort of man before. Trent wasn't bulky or anything. But he had calluses on his palms and muscles in places where she'd had no idea...

Instead of lying down beside her, he detoured to the dresser and pulled a box of condoms from the drawer. He took out a packet, then moved the box to the nightstand. She grinned at his optimism. He responded in kind before crawling onto the bed and kissing her shoulder.

"I like your smile," he said in a husky whisper and cupped a breast. He pressed a kiss just above her beaded nipple, then licked it with a slow flat tongue.

Gasping softly, she automatically rolled toward him, seeking more. Needing more. After another leisurely swipe, he sucked the entire nipple into his mouth. She was holding her breath again. This time, she let it out slowly and closed her eyes when he moved a hand down her body, following the curve of her hip, then ending the return trip at the protective seam of her thighs.

He tried to slide in his fingers, but she wasn't ready to come apart yet.

"Hey."

"Patience," she said, liking the way she was making him crazy.

She felt his chest move as he groaned. Oh, she had no doubt he would take her to that place she ached for...and he could accomplish it quickly. But first, she had her own exploring to do.

Starting with his left pec, she skimmed her palm over the swell of flesh and muscle, over his flat nipple. Obviously it wasn't sensitive. She tried the right one…

Trent's low gravelly chuckle stroked every sensitive inch of her body as effectively as if he'd used his hand and tongue on her.

"Ticklish?" With a coy peek through her lashes, she blew on the puckering brown nub.

"Only there."

"Good to know."

"Better think real hard before striking that match." A faint smile touched the corners of his mouth. "Little city girls shouldn't play with fire."

Shelby laughed and pretended the dark intent in his eyes wasn't hot enough to short-circuit her entire system. Wrapping her hand around his erection, she said, "Ready to change your tune?"

His cock jerked. The sound he made was part laugh, but mostly groan. She stroked upward, increasing the pressure, loving the feel of the hot smooth flesh pulsing in her grasp.

On a ragged exhale, he caught her wrist, pulled her hand away, and pinned her shoulders to the mattress. His face loomed just above hers, his eyes glittering with challenge, and his smile utterly wicked when he threw a leg over her, immobilizing her hips. Almost. She still had wiggle room. A slight move to the right brushed his cock and had him clenching his jaw.

"Why don't you want me to touch you?" she asked.

"I never said that." He lowered his mouth to her jaw and kissed his way to her ear.

"You pushed me away when I'd just gotten started."

"Don't pretend you don't know why," he murmured and bit her earlobe.

"Hey," she muttered, even though the light nip felt good.

He shut her up with an openmouthed kiss that made her squeeze her thighs more tightly together. He kneaded her breast gently, then teased it with his fingers while kissing her breathless.

Her skin felt cool from the light breeze sneaking in the open window, yet she felt burning hot wherever their bodies touched. She broke the kiss for some much-needed air.

Trent lowered his head. He took one of her nipples into his mouth and sucked deeply.

She arched off the mattress and clutched at the sheets, only then realizing she had a free hand. He still held the other one captive.

He switched to the other breast, giving it equal attention, before trailing kisses down to her belly. Every time his erection brushed against her hip or leg, he jerked a little. She did her best to make that happen a lot.

His patience was astounding. She wouldn't have guessed he'd be the type to stretch foreplay out this long. Everything he'd been doing felt amazing. But right now she was feeling needy, greedy and edgy, the hunger inside her going bone-deep. It was a little scary. For God's sake she didn't want to end up begging.

He circled her belly button with the tip of his tongue. He'd moved his hand to her breast, the other molded her hip. She rubbed his shoulder, still in awe of his physique. She traced a muscle over to his back. Whimpered when he thumbed her aching nipple. He shifted and turned away, fueling her frustration.

"Oh, for… Do I have to keep fantasizing about how you'll feel inside me, or are you going to get on with it?"

That's when she realized he was only getting the condom.

He looked at her with an expression of amazement before he laughed. Blushing, she couldn't believe what she'd just said. Out loud. God.

No, she would not cover her face.

"You'll have to unlock Fort Knox first," he said with a nod at her clamped thighs.

"Ha. Funny." She saw that he was as hard as ever. And more beautiful than she'd imagined.

He tore the packet open. "I want to do everything all at once."

"Uh…I don't think that's possible," she said, watching him put on the condom, her breath catching.

"I bet you want to be on top."

"I don't actually care," she said, "as long as I get to see your face."

He lowered his head. "I think I can arrange that," he said and moved between her legs. "Do you have any idea how badly I want you?"

At his raspy admission her whole body tingled. "So I'm not the only one, huh?"

He inhaled deeply, as the look in his eyes softened, grew warmer. "No, you are not." He kissed her lightly, and she could feel how he was trembling. How he was trying to hold back and not overwhelm her.

Seconds later, he slid two fingers inside her, and she spasmed around them, her moan louder than she'd expected.

"You're perfect," he said, using his fingers to tease her and his thumb to drive her crazy.

"Now would be a good time to, you know—"

His fingers slipped out, but his thumb kept circling and circling. "So, you're saying you think now would be a good time for me to—you know. Right?"

"When this is over, I'm going to kill you, Trent Ki—"

He thrust inside her all in one go. And then he kept

thrusting, never losing his rhythm as he lifted her left leg and settled it over his shoulder.

Somehow, his thumb had never wavered. He'd even softened the pressure, as if he could read her body like a book.

Her breathing had become panting, her thoughts reduced to begging and her grip on him had to hurt. But none of that mattered because she was going to come any second. Every muscle in her body tightened, and it was clear he wasn't going to last, either.

As hard as she tried to keep her eyes open, to watch him unravel, they closed as she climaxed. As her world became nothing but shimmering sensation, wave after wave of sheer, unrelenting pleasure.

He touched her cheek, then trailed down to her breast with an unsteady hand. She clenched her muscles around his erection, rocked her hips.

His raw, feral groan forced her eyes open.

Trent was arched above her, his neck corded, his muscles straining. He was the most gorgeous man she'd ever seen, and she wanted to remember this forever.

When he finally came down, he pulled out of her before he flopped to her side. She was still learning how to breathe again, as the aftershocks kept surprising the breath out of her.

"I never expected…this," he whispered.

She knew just what he meant. "Me, neither."

"Well, hell," he said.

All Shelby could do was nod.

# *13*

SHELBY WASN'T NEXT to him when Trent woke up shortly after sunrise. He knew she must've left his bed some-time after midnight. They'd been awake until then, mak-ing out like a couple of horny teenagers. Hell, he couldn't even remember the last time he'd needed three condoms in one night.

He saw that her bedroom door was slightly ajar when he slipped into the bathroom. He thought he heard her moving around in the kitchen so he listened to be certain before going about his business. It sure would be great if she was making coffee. Normally he got it ready the evening be-fore and programmed the timer. But there'd been nothing routine about last night. They'd barely made it up for air.

Shelby was amazing. Beautiful, smart, kind. Talented. In a lot more ways than he should be thinking about right now. He turned on the shower and pressed the heel of his hand down on his erection. For some reason he decided greeting her with a hard-on might not be the smoothest move.

They'd stayed clear of conversations about the ranch or anything else of importance last night. He didn't regret one minute. But two things hadn't changed. Shelby was fresh off a relationship that had gone sour, and sooner or later she'd discover she had no claim to the Eager Beaver. He dreaded that day as much as he did a trip to the dentist. That was saying something considering his phobia.

He finished his shower and got dressed, hoping like hell that when he entered the kitchen, he wouldn't walk headfirst into a wall of regret. The second he opened the bathroom door he smelled coffee.

Shelby was standing at the sink with damp hair, dressed in jeans and a pink blouse, her back to him.

Hoping not to startle her, he said, "Good morning."

She jumped anyway, before turning with a smile. "Hey."

A part of him wanted to walk right up and kiss her. But instinct kept him in check. She seemed a little stiff. Yet she'd set his mug on the counter for him.

"Thanks for making coffee."

"I don't know if it's strong enough. I used two scoops."

"Great." He liked three, but he'd drink it any way she made it.

She sipped from her own mug and watched him pour the brew into his. He took his time adding some sugar from the white canister next to the coffeemaker. The sudden silence felt awkward. He'd been leery of how things would go between them, but he hadn't expected this.

He gave his coffee a brief stir and left it on the counter. Dammit. This sucked. He looked at her. "I want to kiss you."

Caught in the middle of a sip, she quickly swallowed and blinked at him. "So what's stopping you?"

Trent laughed, mostly at himself. Taking her mug out of her hand, he set it on the counter next to his. A light tug and she stepped into his arms.

Her lips were soft and yielding as he took his time, rubbing a hand down her back, enjoying her warmth and womanly curves. Today she smelled like peaches. That was something new. Probably her shampoo. Her skin just smelled clean and sweet. He waited until she parted her lips in invitation before he used his tongue. And promised himself he wouldn't get carried away.

Not anything he needed to worry about, apparently. Shelby let him have a little taste, then broke the kiss and stepped back. She lowered the hand that had been placed lightly on his chest.

"I have a lot of work to do today," she said, her gaze flickering.

"We both do." He picked up his coffee and gulped. Damn, it was hot. "After I drink this I'll go tend to Daisy."

"I'm supposed to do the milking—"

"You can have a break."

"No, you don't have to…" She bit her lip. "Look, last night was really—"

"Great," he finished to ease her look of distress. "For me at least. But you don't want it to happen again. I get it." He lifted a shoulder in a deceptively casual shrug. "It's okay."

"No. It's not that." She cleared her throat. "It's just— well, we hadn't talked. You know, before getting carried away and all…" Her voice trailed off and she turned her gaze to the window.

Trent sighed.

"See?" She darted him a glance. "This is exactly what I mean."

"What?"

"That sigh." A blush stained her cheeks. "You think I have expectations. But I don't. Last night *was* great. Better than great for me." A tiny smile teased the corners of her lips and then she slumped. "We should've set the record straight first."

"Shelby, I sighed because you can barely look at me." He set down his mug, his eyes staying on her face. "I hate seeing you uncomfortable. And for that record of yours, not once did it occur to me you'd have expectations."

She blinked, then studied him. "What about you?"

"Me? Expectations? No." He shook his head. "Hopes and dreams? Definitely." She laughed and his mood brightened. He tried for her hand and caught her fingertips. "Better than great, huh?"

She leveled him with a mock glare. "That doesn't mean we're going to screw like bunnies."

"Okay," he said with a solemn nod. It wasn't easy. He tugged on two fingers, urging her closer. She took a step forward, and so did he.

Trent put his arms around her and she looped hers around his neck. He kissed the sweet spot behind her ear, smiling at the predictable shiver rippling through her body. "After I tend to Daisy, I'll make us some breakfast," he said, and brushed another kiss a little lower. "How's that?"

"You must be starving."

"Oh, I am." He bit her earlobe.

"I meant because we skipped dinner."

"That's all I meant, too."

She leaned back to look at him. He made sure he was the picture of innocence. Except he was getting hard and he knew by her raised brows the instant she felt it.

"Ignore everything due south. This will be only a kiss. I promise."

Shelby smiled just before their lips met. He couldn't help grinning in response, which made for a pretty lousy kiss. Neither of them complained. They got right back on track, as if their lips and tongues had been doing the same dance together for a whole lifetime. A troubling thought to some degree.

They were getting warmed up real nice when Shelby stiffened suddenly. "The movers..." she said, drawing back, eyes wide. "They're coming this morning and I'm not ready for them."

"What do you have to do?" he asked, the reminder forcing him to think about something he should've considered before having sex with her.

He didn't try to hold on to her. Without a doubt, he knew he had Shelby's best interests at heart by keeping his promise to Violet. It was possible Shelby wouldn't see it that way. Eventually she'd find out she had no stake in the ranch. And that he'd known before the movers had arrived, before they'd slept together. And when she did find out, he'd damn well better be the one who told her.

AFTER SHELBY EMPTIED the fourth box, she carefully broke down the cardboard and laid it on the pile by her bedroom door. She wouldn't unpack everything, not yet. Just some winter clothes, a few kitchen items and the rest of her jewelry supplies. She hadn't tried to find her grandfather's will. By itself the document meant very little. What Violet had confided about the ranch yesterday still weighed on Shelby. Especially after last night.

While there was no telling if Violet was delusional, or had any ability to determine who owned the Eager Beaver, it still felt wrong not to tell Trent. Thank goodness for the promise Shelby had made. At least she could fall back on that if things got dicey. Of course that made her somewhat of a coward. But after the glorious night they'd shared, it was going to kill her to see the look on his face if he learned the ranch didn't belong to him or his family. Another eight or nine days without being sure would be torture enough, but then they'd have to get through three months together. Boy, that had certainly sounded like a better deal a couple of days ago.

Why couldn't Violet have waited until she had proof

before saying anything? Somehow Shelby felt quite sure Violet wasn't trying to cause trouble.

But she had to stop thinking about Violet, the ranch and even Trent if she could. It was great to have her things within reach. Most of it was stored in the shed, but only because she'd started working in the third room. Trent had insisted she use the space and even moved the few boxes he'd kept in there.

They'd found a spot in the living room for her over-stuffed reading chair but her couch was outside. The shed was the most logical place to store the big items. She'd even decided to put her bed in there. But only after she was certain Trent understood the decision was not a state-ment about their new sex life. Using the smaller daybed simply made more sense.

Remembering his feeble attempt to control a smile while she'd explained her reasoning made her shake her head. How could a man be so irritating and endearing at the same time? The way he slid back and forth between the professional horse trainer and the simple cowboy still amused her. Trent was one of a kind. She really liked him, dammit. Twice she'd made a special trip to the kitchen just to peek out the window and watch him work with Solomon.

That baloney had to stop. She had so much of her own work to do.

The county fair would be opening before she knew it, and with only two dozen pairs of earrings and fifteen neck-laces in her inventory she was right to be concerned.

God, what if she couldn't sell a single piece?

Her stomach knotted. She shoved the harmful thought aside. She didn't know the area or the people who lived around Blackfoot Falls. Her work might not appeal to them so it wasn't wrong to be prepared for the worst. Of course she'd be disappointed but she couldn't afford self-doubt. Her jewelry had been popular right up until Donald's family had made her stop making them. There had to be a market for her designs somewhere. Her best bet might end up being to sell the jewelry online.

She hung up a few sweaters, glanced at her dresser standing in the corner and did a little happy dance. Who would've thought she could be so excited about having real drawers? Her gaze caught on the digital clock sitting on top. Midafternoon already and she hadn't gotten to work yet.

"Shelby?" Trent stood at her door. His voice alone sent her heart into a somersault. The way he smiled at her curled her toes. "Can you come for a minute?"

"Sure." She stepped over bags of toiletries and miscellaneous items she needed to go through later. "What's going on?"

"I'll show you," he said, holding out his hand.

"Can't you tell me?"

"Nope."

"You're being cryptic."

"Yep."

She laughed at his lopsided smile and let his hand close around hers. It felt weirdly right and safe to be led all the way to the barn without him letting go even once. Safe, and perhaps a little too comfortable.

This wasn't her standing on her own, forging a new path into the future.

Oh, for God's sake. Sometimes she drove herself crazy. In the grand scheme of things, the two of them were the proverbial ships in the night. Her new life had begun the day she'd left Denver. Trent was a bonus she hadn't expected. And she needed to shut up and enjoy him for as long as things lasted between them.

"We'll have to be quiet," he whispered as they disappeared into the shadows at the far back.

She heard something. Soft yet high-pitched, almost a whine.

"Wha—?" A silencing finger touched her lips.

A few more feet and they stopped. He slipped behind her and wrapped her in his arms, so that she leaned back against his chest. He ducked his head to her level and pointed to a short stack of hay bales.

Mostly it was dark and her eyes were still adjusting. Seeping through narrow gaps in the wall the dappled sunlight helped. Shelby squinted, listened. Was that a cat between the wall and the hay? With a whole bunch of tiny kittens?

A soft gasp escaped her. She clamped her mouth shut.

Trent pressed his cheek to hers, and she felt him smile.

Mama had spotted them, her eyes green and glowing in the murky light, piercing them with a warning glare. Her tail shot high and twitched. Probably the feline version of giving them the finger for disturbing her babies. Shelby really didn't know much about cats.

"They're only a few hours old," Trent said, keeping his voice low.

"I didn't know you had a cat. What's her name?"

"She's not mine."

"Then whose?"

"She's feral. I might've fed her a few times," he said, straightening. "Hell, I've been calling her Tom. Should've known it was another female."

Shelby turned to grin at him. "Oh, poor Trent. Surrounded by women. You have Mutt."

"Yeah, right. The traitor."

"Mutt?"

"He's been wanting to sleep with you since the day you showed up. At least I beat him to it."

"You did not just say that."

He smiled and motioned with his head for them to leave.

"I'll check on them throughout the day," he said, keeping an arm around her shoulders as they exited the barn. "They should be okay."

"Could you tell how many kittens?"

"Five, I think. You going to finish unpacking?"

"Maybe this evening. I have to get to work." She sensed his disappointment. "So I can knock off at a decent hour."

He didn't react as she'd hoped. Just lowered his arm and nodded. "Me, too. I have some repairs to make on the east corral. I heard we might be getting some cold temperatures."

"Oh, no. What about the fair?"

"The weekend's supposed to be fine. They're predicting the cold front to hit on Monday."

"Snow?"

"I hope not. I might have to buy a new winter jacket. Living in Texas for ten years spoiled me."

"That's one reason I was so relieved to get my things. I have a ton of sweatshirts and sweaters. It would've killed me to spend a penny on clothes." They stopped at the porch steps. "It's not that I'm a cheapskate," she said, looking up into his steady gaze, her heart beginning to pound. "I'll be putting a lot of money into supplies. Beads are cheap, but silver isn't. I ordered a soldering iron online yesterday, which will probably take at least ten days to arrive. Plus I need a new torch, a good backup supply of soldering picks and silver wire… Sorry, I don't know why I'm rambling. Too much on my mind." They both just stood there. "Are you coming inside?"

"Not unless you need my help moving something."

"No, not really." She should be glad he was staying outside. Otherwise he'd be a distraction. "I can make coffee so you can fill your thermos."

"I still have some." He pressed his lips together, something hot and unmistakable flaring in his eyes. Trent wanted to kiss her. She'd bet he wanted to do more than that, and holy crap, she doubted she could refuse. "Call if you need me," he said, his voice and expression too neutral to not mean something. So what was he trying to hide? "I'll be in the stable or the corral."

"Thanks." She smiled, and as soon as he made a move to go she stepped onto the porch, telling herself she wouldn't look back.

Her willpower carried her into the house. Once inside she peered out the screen door, watching him walk to the stable. Even his stride seemed a bit off. His demeanor had shifted in a matter of seconds. Shelby was pretty sure something important had just happened. She just didn't know what it was.

# 14

WHEN SHELBY'S GLUE gun died on her, she decided to call it quits for the day. She had another one somewhere but this was her favorite. Working without a spare made her nervous so she'd have to check with the variety store in town or place another order online. Also, discovering that she'd outgrown working with beads, colored glass and the occasional feather or shell was dampening her enthusiasm.

She should've known better. Back in college, earrings made from those kinds of materials had been her bread and butter. But after working for the Williamsons, she'd come too far from her early days of experimenting with cheaper supplies.

And she had to admit she'd become accustomed to cushier work. Designing expensive baubles was a whole lot easier than getting her hands dirty and bending over a work table all day.

She pressed a hand to her lower back, applying pressure in increments, and glanced at the clock. It was so late she forgot about the slight ache. How could she have worked five hours straight?

Oh, well, she was still itching to get her hands on the bigger torch she hadn't been able to afford in college. With it she'd be able to work with hard-grade silver, something she hadn't done yet.

She washed her hands in the bathroom sink before heading for the kitchen. Trent sat at the table watching something on his laptop. A quick peek told her it wasn't the same video of Race the Moon. However, she caught a glimpse of a different horse and rider on a racetrack.

But it was the breadth of Trent's shoulders that held her attention. And the way his thick dark hair tended to curl at his nape. The silky texture had surprised her, and now the memory had her fisting her hands to keep from touching him.

Hoping she wouldn't disturb him, she continued quietly to the fridge. Not counting the apple she'd gobbled earlier, she'd missed lunch and hadn't given a single thought to dinner.

"Hey, you." Trent leaned back in his chair, his head angled toward her. "Are you finished working?"

"Yep, the staff mutinied." Nothing quick and easy in the fridge, but she noticed a pot sitting on the stove. "My glue gun quit on me. Think I can find one at the variety store?"

"Maybe." His gaze roamed her face, lowered to her chest and hips, his mouth curving in a faint smile. Because of her Tweety Bird T-shirt, perhaps, but she didn't think so. Wrong sort of smile, judging by her accelerated pulse. "If not, try the fabric shop."

"Have you eaten?"

"I was waiting for you. There's chili from the freezer in the pot on the stove," he said, and followed her gaze to the computer screen. "Calhoun emailed me this video."

"Oh." Weird. "Did you change your mind about working for him?"

"Nah. He's still trying to sell me on the Arabian. I'm just drooling over his setup. The guy might be a jerk but his stables and racetrack are primo."

"You have a lot of land for a track. Can't you—" She remembered the precise thing she'd been trying to forget. For the time being, anyway. Why had Violet told her? Surely the woman could've waited for confirmation on who owned the Eager Beaver. Knowing what little she did, Shelby somehow felt as if she was betraying Trent. He was giving her a curious look, so she shrugged. "Ignore me. What do I know about horses and racetracks?"

"Ignore you?" He snorted a laugh. "Sure, I'll just go grab a pair of blinders from the stable."

Grinning, she got a glass out of the cabinet, then paused. "Want anything?"

He stared long enough for her to get that he had sex on the brain, before refocusing on the laptop. "A training facility is more complicated and costly than you might think. Racehorses are valuable animals. Some of them are insured for millions. You gotta treat them with kid gloves." He looked back at her. "You visit the stable yet?"

"Only once, briefly." She'd been amazed at the pristine condition inside.

"You won't find a single hinge or latch with a sharp edge or a bolt sticking out. I had the stall doors custom-made and so far I've replaced half the barbed-wire fence in the north pasture with solid wood. Even with all the money I've sunk into the place and work I've done myself, I couldn't board and train horses yet. Still too many hazards around here. Solomon's mine and he's safe. I paid a nice sum for him out of a bonus a couple years back. And Jax, it's looking as if he'll never race. Good all-around horse, though."

"What about Griffin?"

He smiled at the name she'd given the colt. "His training is coming along fine. He's got potential. It won't be long before I can take him to the track outside of Kalispell, the same one I use for Solomon." He shrugged. "I start making some good money again with Solomon or training, and who knows? I can get this place up to standard."

Shelby's stomach churned. Listening to how much time and money Trent had invested made her sick. Even if Violet was right about the Eager Beaver, Shelby would never ask him to leave. Surely, they could work something out.

No. Even after a brief acquaintance, she knew Trent had too much pride. He wouldn't stick around. The best she could do would be to repay him for the improvements he'd made. Though it would probably take her years.

"Why the sad face?"

She shrugged it off and poured herself some water.

His expression troubled, he stood. He took her glass, set it on the counter and put his arms around her. Held her close. "It's about the Eager Beaver, isn't it?"

Her whole body tensed. "What do you mean?"

"It's a touchy subject for both of us. I say we ban any mention of the ranch." He rubbed her back, and she hid her face against his chest. "What happens, happens. We'll deal with it when the time comes. No matter what, we have a grace period agreement. Right?"

What else could she do but nod?

He leaned back. "I make a mean chili," he said, and nudged her chin up. "How about it?"

Shelby met his sympathetic eyes. "I thought you couldn't cook."

"I can't. That's why there's leftovers." He smiled that damn cute-boy smile. It got to her almost as much as the sexy version. "I figure we're both hungry enough it won't taste too bad."

She couldn't help laughing. "I'm in."

His eyes had already begun to darken. He'd lifted his hand to stroke her hair. Clearly he had dessert planned, as well. Fine with her. She'd grab some of that good loving while he was still offering.

And try not to dwell on their looming expiration date.

"UNPACKING OR RELAXING?" Trent asked the second he dumped the clean pot on the draining rack.

They'd worked together, he washing and she drying, only because she'd insisted. He didn't see the point—he usually just let the dishes air-dry—but he hadn't argued. Though now, he blocked her reach for the pot.

"We're gonna let that one dry all by itself," he said, taking the towel from her and tossing it on the counter.

Shelby opened her mouth to object and he swooped in for a kiss. She sputtered in surprise but settled quickly, and let him have his way with her. Giving as good as she got, and then some.

He couldn't believe he'd gotten so hard so fast. Jesus, there was nothing remotely hot about a sudsy pot. But knowing what came next had lit a fire in his belly before he'd so much as touched Shelby. He figured her pretty lips and laughing green eyes might've played a small part.

He skimmed a hand over the curve of her firm, round backside and deepened the kiss. The little moaning sound she made was sexy as hell, tempting him to pick her up and carry her caveman-style straight to his bed. Suspecting she might have a problem with that, he kept kissing her instead.

She slid her hands up to his shoulders and pressed her soft breasts against his chest. He could almost taste the ripeness of those perfect rosy tips. Damn, the woman was responsive. He'd bet she was good and wet already, and sweet as honey.

Their tongues tangled. She pressed closer, rubbing her belly and hips against his fly, forcing his cock to take notice. As if it wasn't already standing at attention. He tensed, resisting the urge to lift her onto the counter and strip off her jeans. But if she kept at it, he wasn't sure he could trust himself. He grabbed a handful of her hair. Pure silk.

Ignoring his slight tug at her scalp, she kept kissing him with an eagerness he found arousing, but also curious. Something was different about her tonight. Damned if he was going to analyze it now. She rocked her hips against him and seemed to make it her mission to taste every inch of his mouth. He released her hair and slid his hands down her spine. No way he'd last long. He squeezed her butt, the pressure inside him building...

Shelby pulled back suddenly. "We're in the kitchen again," she said, her voice a breathless whisper.

"I know." He tightened his arms, needing to feel her against him.

"Must be a fetish."

He paused to look at her. "Me?"

Trying to catch her breath, she laughed. "Same problem as last night. Violet, remember?"

Trent fixated on her distracting lower lip. It was Tuesday. For sure Violet was glued to the TV. "We'll move. In a minute." He cupped her face between his hands and paid homage to her lips.

"Or Jimmy," she murmured against his mouth. "He could—"

*Jimmy?*

The thought cooled him. Yeah, he didn't need the kid popping up unexpectedly and getting an eyeful. Especially with Trent not being at his smoothest. It was Shelby's fault. She had him so turned on he hadn't felt more awkward since his first time at sixteen.

He patted her fanny. "Let's go."

Shelby made no move. Humor shined in her eyes. "You're more worried about Jimmy seeing us."

"No, I'm not." Trent backed her to the door and turned her around.

She grinned over her shoulder at him. "Why?"

Trent just shook his head.

"Huh. Must be a guy thing."

"Probably." He tried to give her backside another tap but she scrambled out of reach.

Mutt barked at the kitchen door.

Shelby turned around.

"Keep going," Trent said. "He's staying outside."

"But—"

"Just for now."

She nodded, walked briskly to the hall and turned left to his bedroom without a word. Following behind, he couldn't help noticing the stack of cardboard outside her door and wondered if she'd dug out her grandfather's will.

Hell would freeze over before he'd ask. Not a subject he wanted to visit. He'd seen her pawing through sweatshirts like it was Christmas. Learning she was counting pennies to support her new business had felt like a two-by-four to the gut. Was she just being frugal? Or did Shelby need the ranch as much as he did?

The eagerness he'd sensed earlier had held a trace of desperation. She knew something had to give soon. And maybe she'd decided, just as he had, that they'd enjoy their time together while they could. Not the ideal situation, but probably the best he could hope for.

She stood at the foot of the bed, her eyes shining, her head tilted a bit to the right. "Did you get lost?"

"I knew you were about to ravage me, so I took a breather."

Her throaty laugh cranked up the heat. "You wish."

Smiling, he tugged up the hem of her shirt. "Am I going to find another weird contraption under here?"

"Maybe." She lifted her arms without him asking.

He drew the shirt over her head and tossed it against

the wall. His gaze stayed on the lacy black bra. "Pretty," he said. "Pity it's gotta come off."

"Wait." She clutched his arm, forestalling his bid for the back hook. After shoving his hand away, she unzipped her jeans and pushed them down her hips. She kicked them aside and stood there, waiting.

He studied the black bikini panties. Remembering vividly what they were hiding, his cock was ready to explode through his fly. His gaze moved up to the bra. "They match. Is that what you wanted me to see?"

Shelby pursed her lips, then slumped on a sigh. "Yes. I was trying to redeem myself after last night. But now I just feel stupid. Thank you."

Trent laughed. "Ah. Sweet, warm, sexy Shelby," he murmured, drawing her into his arms and inhaling her skin and hair. "I'll let you in on a secret. You didn't have to do a damn thing for me to want you like crazy." One flick freed the bra's clasp.

When she yanked up his shirt, he was more than happy to give her a hand. They were both naked in less than a minute.

Flushed and warm, her skin was a soft pink, all except for her small tight nipples. He rubbed both thumbs over the darker, rosier tips, and felt her tremble. Placing a hand on his forearm to steady herself, she tried to stand still, barely moving when he bowed his head for a taste. He licked both nipples, then sucked the left one until she wouldn't stop squirming.

He brushed a kiss across her lips as he straightened. Her eyes looked almost black.

Not bothering with the quilt, he walked her backward until she bumped into the bed. A gentle hand on her shoulder was all it took for her to sink to the edge of the mattress.

"Condoms," she reminded him, her breath hitching.

"We don't need them yet." He crouched and spread her legs.

With a soft gasp, she fell back, supporting herself on her elbows while she watched him kiss the inside of her thigh. Her skin was as smooth and soft as satin. He switched to her other thigh, planted a quicker kiss there, too anxious to get to the wet heat in between. He parted her lips with his fingers, then followed with his tongue.

She bucked against his mouth. Her breathy moans drove him crazy. He sucked and licked and thrust his tongue as far as he could, unable to get enough. She kept moving, breaking contact with his mouth, finally going still when he inserted two fingers inside her. He repositioned himself and when she began bucking again, he stayed with her. Within seconds she climaxed, her orgasm quaking through her flushed body.

Cursing himself for not having the condom closer, he got up to grab the packet. He forced himself to unwrap it carefully while he watched Shelby. The way she was arching and moaning only made him more impatient. But she was watching him, too, and she dragged herself back toward the pillows, getting ready for him.

Trent propped himself on one arm and caressed her cheek. Her eyes fluttered closed and with a single thrust, he entered her, fast and deep. He caught her gasp in his mouth and kissed her as thoroughly as possible, considering he was about to explode. Lifting his head, he looked into her dazed eyes.

He pulled out, shifted, hoping to make every move count, give her as much pleasure as possible. Bringing her leg up higher around his waist he sunk into her. By her moan he knew he'd found the perfect angle. Keeping control of himself was the problem.

Arching up to reach him, she raked her fingernails down his chest. The way she'd moved drove him deeper, making her moan louder. He stilled, cupped her breast, then leaned down to kiss her parted lips. On his way back up he stopped briefly to suck her nipple.

Then he tried out their new position with another hard thrust.

Her shoulders came up off the mattress again. She murmured something he didn't catch, then shifted her hips to the right and nearly set him off.

He slowly withdrew, smiling at her cute pout.

"Don't you dare," she panted, clutching at his arms, trying to pull him back to her. "Trent, please."

For a long time they stared into each other's eyes, and then he entered her again and started moving. Slowly at first, before thrusting harder, deeper until she writhed and whimpered, and then bucked up against him as she came. He bent to kiss her and she squeezed him so hard it triggered his own explosive release.

## 15

THE WEATHER WAS PERFECT the first day of the fair. With the cooler temperatures, it finally was beginning to feel like fall, Shelby's favorite season. Good for long sleeves, but no jacket needed during the day. The gorgeous blue sky stretched all the way to the distant Rockies where most of the clouds hovered. She was lucky her booth faced that direction.

A line of cars turning off the highway caught her attention and she checked her watch. The fair officially opened in fifteen minutes. Trent had set up the tables and secured the awning for shade while she'd unpacked her jewelry and laid everything out, so she'd been ready for an hour. She appreciated his help, but it had given her extra time to fret.

Sighing, she glanced at the earrings and necklaces she'd placed on the center table. At first she'd worried about her meager inventory. The booth on her left overflowed with homemade baked goods and to her right a friendly older woman was selling beautiful porcelain dolls. Considering Gladys had made each intricate doll herself, she offered quite a variety.

But then it occurred to Shelby that having less jewelry on display meant she wouldn't be so mortified when she didn't sell squat. People might think she'd sold out quickly. The rationale had cheered her some. Though she was still tense. And Trent telling her all morning not to be nervous didn't make her any less so.

Wondering what was keeping him, she poked her head out. She spotted him in front of the cotton-candy wagon, holding the drinks he'd gone to get them and talking to a young couple. She swore the man knew everyone.

She got a whiff of popcorn and pressed a hand to her roiling tummy. Other food smells were beginning to permeate the air. Great. She tried to distract herself by scanning the kiddie rides being tested just past the row of food vendors. Not a good idea. She was terrible at fairs and festivals, wanting every fried and sugar-coated treat in sight. And she usually gave in.

"Sorry I took so long. I kept running into—" Trent lowered the cup he'd been about to pass her. "You don't look so hot."

"Just nerves." She waved dismissively and peered at the cup. "What did you get?"

"Hot chocolate."

"Ah." No, she'd have to wait on that. Her stomach would rebel for sure.

He set the two cups aside. "Shelby." He placed his hands on her shoulders and gave her a warm smile. "It's going to be fine."

"I know." She shrugged. "I'm being ridiculous."

"I didn't say that." He ran his hands down her arms and pulled her close. Obviously he didn't have a problem with people seeing them together like this.

She didn't, either, but she still glanced around.

"Even giving myself a ten-percent margin for bias, your jewelry is terrific. I don't understand where this insecurity is coming from."

Her eyes burned a little at his praise. She wanted to

stay right where she was, her face half buried in his chest until they could leave. "I wish I'd had the time and supplies to make better stuff. Some of this goes back to my college days. I only brought them because I was desperate." She drew back. "Sadie was so nice to rent me a booth. I couldn't sit here with nothing. But honestly, I really should've thrown some of this junk out or donated it by now."

Frowning, he took a long considering look at her, and then at the displays. "You're not seeing clearly. I don't see any junk here." He sounded a bit put-off. Probably sick of her self-pity, and she didn't blame him.

Clearing her throat, she straightened, smiled. "You're right. I told you I was being ridiculous."

He obviously wasn't buying her born-again act. A scowl darkened his face. "I'd sure like five minutes alone with the person who did a number on you."

"What? No. I'm a very good designer. I know that. For God's sake, I've designed rings and necklaces for celebrities from all over the country. It's just—" She sighed. "I haven't done this sort of work in a while."

Still troubled, he opened his mouth to say something but someone called out to him.

"Trent Kimball. I thought that was you. It's been a long while." The stout graying woman displaying lovely handmade quilts down the way from them strolled over. "How are your folks doing?"

"Fine," he said. "Just fine. And yourself, Mrs. Stanley?"

"Can't complain. Retirement has its ups and downs."

"I imagine so." To Shelby he said, "Mrs. Stanley was my sixth-grade teacher." He made a quick introduction, and Shelby managed to get out a hello before a throng of people coming toward them sent Mrs. Stanley scurrying back to her booth.

The crowd swelled and thinned for the next three hours.

Trent stayed with her a good deal of the time, when he wasn't being pulled away to the cavernous warehouse-looking building where horses and other livestock were being judged for one thing or another.

A cute girl in her early teens challenged him to enter the pie-eating contest. He'd only laughed. When her pushing went from cute to bothersome he'd told her, in no uncertain terms, it wasn't going to happen. Shelby would never tell Trent, but she understood why the girl had been so insistent. Or that half the women at the fair had given him a twice-over. And the other half needed glasses.

Shelby heard there would be a junior rodeo later in the evening. At the same time tomorrow was the much-anticipated demolition derby with a five-thousand-dollar prize going to the person who took first place. The event was sold out, Gladys had told her, so the crowd would be bigger tomorrow evening. Apparently Gladys's sales were in line with Shelby's, as in pathetic.

The good news was, her stomach had settled down. In the bad news column—out of boredom, she'd eaten a hot dog, half an order of disgusting nachos, a frozen lemonade and three chocolate-chip cookies from the booth on the other side of her. Now she was contemplating a funnel cake. If all that food made her sick, at least she'd have an excuse to go home.

"Here you are. How are you doing?"

Shelby turned, pleased to see it was Sadie. "Okay. Did you just get here?"

"Nah, a couple hours ago." She inclined her head toward the building. "Putting out fires. You'd think some of those cocky hotheads were putting their private parts on display instead of their livestock."

Shelby laughed. "Men."

"Amen, sister." Sadie reached for a pair of earrings and

held them up. Dangling from a brass crescent moon, three strings of glass beads caught the late sun. "This is pretty."

Biting her lip, Shelby said nothing. The three times she'd seen the woman, Sadie hadn't worn jewelry. She was just being nice. It made Shelby feel worse.

"Oh, look at these." She held up another similar pair, only with a brass sun, and the longer beads a mix of purple and gold. "I'll take them both," she said and pulled out money from the neckline of her yellow knit top.

"You don't have pierced ears," Shelby said.

Sadie snorted. "They aren't for me. I don't wear jewelry. My daughter and granddaughter will love 'em in their Christmas stockings. Purple and gold are Julie's school colors. How much do I owe you?"

Shelby forced a smile. "The price should be on the back of the card."

Sadie turned it over and frowned.

"Too much?" Shelby searched her pockets for the pen. "I can reduce it."

"Had to cost you more than this for the material." Sadie passed the earrings to her. "Better check the others. Make sure you didn't make a mistake with them, too."

Shelby stared at the price. "I guess I wasn't thinking," she murmured. "Please. Pay me what's marked. That's fair." She quickly wrapped the earrings in white tissue paper. "I'll check the other prices."

"Be sure that you do," Sadie said, with a glance toward the parking area. "These first few hours are always slow. People are knocking off work about now and trust me, pretty soon they'll be here in droves." Sadie accepted the wrapped earrings and passed over the money. "It's the correct amount. No change. See you later, hon."

Shelby fisted the bills, knowing full well that Sadie had paid her too much. But calling her on it would likely create a scene. Last thing Shelby wanted. The sun was sinking, leaving her to decide on a new spot for her folding chair.

She thought about Sadie's advice on the pricing, and admitted she was probably right. Shelby was out of touch with the real world. People who had money rarely cared about what baubles cost, especially if they were meant to impress.

First she found her pen, then quickly scanned the stickers and tried to make reasonable price adjustments. Something made her look up. Trent was headed toward the booth, tall, posture straight and looking ridiculously hot in dark jeans, a tan Western-cut shirt and brown Stetson.

Of course someone stopped him to talk, but in less than a minute he was walking right to her, a smile on his handsome face. Just watching him made her skin tingle.

"Better be careful, young lady," he said, his voice low and gravelly, moving in so close he forced her to tilt her head back to look at him. "Eyeing a man like that could give him the wrong idea."

"Or the right one."

Grinning, he pushed back the rim of his hat and briefly kissed her. "How've you been doing?" Without waiting for an answer, he swooped in for another brush across her lips.

Sighing, she drew back, her gaze fastened to his. "People are probably watching."

"Let 'em."

She ducked back, placing a refraining hand on his chest. "I should tell you…I signed you up for the chili cook-off."

His confused frown quickly turned into a smile. "Very funny. I seem to remember you cleaning your plate."

"I'm not complaining. But you're a much better kisser than a cook."

"There you go." Their lips barely touched.

"Trent Kimball, quit bothering that poor woman and let her sell her wares."

Evidently he recognized the voice. "Rachel McAllister," he said, before turning to the woman with gorgeous auburn hair. "Still causing trouble."

"It's not McAllister anymore, smart-ass." She was about Shelby's age, close to the same height. Her laughing eyes and friendly smile made Shelby like her instantly.

"That's right. I heard you roped some poor bastard into marrying you."

"Poor bastard," Rachel repeated in a deadpan voice. "Matt's the luckiest guy in the world." She jerked a thumb at the building. "Go ask him."

The blonde woman accompanying her smiled, but kept sifting through the necklaces.

"He must be helping out with the junior rodeo tonight," Trent said, then as an aside to Shelby, "I don't know if you follow rodeo. Matt Gunderson is a champion bull rider." He introduced her to Rachel.

Then Rachel introduced the blonde woman as Jamie. She was married to Cole, Rachel's older brother. Trent seemed to know the whole family. They mentioned the Sundance, which sounded familiar, and then Shelby remembered it was the dude ranch Abe at the variety store had mentioned. Had it really been two weeks already? Wow.

"I would've invited you to the wedding, but I didn't hear you were back until a week later." Rachel was saying when Shelby rejoined the conversation. "Why didn't you tell anybody?"

"I got here in March, just in time for that last snow. The Eager Beaver needed a lot of work before I could settle in. I barely had time to breathe."

"You should've called," Rachel said. "You know my brothers. They would've been right there to give you a hand."

Shelby felt her chest knotting. She didn't know how

much longer she could last keeping Violet's claim from Trent. Aware of Rachel's gaze on her, Shelby wasn't sure if she'd turned as green as she suddenly felt or if it was just curiosity on Rachel's part.

"These are really nice," Jamie said, holding up a necklace. "Did you make these, Shelby?"

She nodded, glad for the diversion. "That's an older piece. I didn't know about the fair in time or I would've had a better selection."

"Are you kidding? These are great." Jamie set the necklace aside and picked up another one.

Rachel's attention turned to the jewelry. "Turquoise." She reached around Jamie for the silver heart-shaped earrings with the turquoise center. "I went to school in Dallas. I love all the turquoise and silver they have in Texas. Wow, these are heavy but really terrific."

Jamie glanced over at them, looking seriously interested.

"Sorry," Rachel told her. "I'm buying them." She scanned the other two tables and picked up another turquoise-and-silver combination.

"Okay, now you're just being a pig," Jamie said, and Rachel laughed. Though Jamie seemed a bit annoyed.

While they continued looking, Shelby slanted a glance at Trent. He stood back, arms crossed, a satisfied smile on his face. Catching her gaze, he winked. If he'd orchestrated this whole thing she was going to kill him.

The two women attracted more shoppers. Within minutes all three tables were crowded with lookers, most of them sifting through the jewelry and asking questions about the different material and stones Shelby used. Whether they bought anything or not, the women all had very nice things to say about Shelby's work.

She kept casting glances at Trent. Most of the time he was engaged in conversation, sometimes with a guy he'd gone to school with or a friend of his parents. Even an old girlfriend of his had stopped to chat. She had a baby on her hip, and two more little ones trailing after her.

The whole time they spoke Trent kept unconsciously loosening his collar, looking more and more like a man relieved he'd dodged a bullet. When the woman finally moved on, he stared after her with an expression of mild shock.

"Do you want kids?" Shelby asked before she'd considered how the question would sound.

He blinked at her, then narrowed his eyes.

She felt a blush and gestured vaguely in the direction of the woman and her children.

"Oh." He removed his hat and ran a hand through his hair. "I think two would be enough."

His gaze intensified when he met her eyes, and she was really, really glad to hear someone say, "Excuse me, miss. I have a question."

For the next two hours, the crowds steadily increased. Trent had wanted to help but there was nothing for him to do except handle the money. He knew so many people, several he hadn't seen in years, so Shelby encouraged him to go catch up with his old friends.

As soon as the rodeo started, the crowd thinned. Shelby had sold a lot and was deciding on whether to follow Gladys's lead and shut down the booth for the night when Rachel showed up.

"Oh, I think Trent's inside," Shelby told her.

"I know. I saw him." She pursed her mouth, looking hesitant. "I have a favor to ask, and if you say no it's fine. I promise. No pressure."

"Okay." Shelby maintained a blank face, convinced things were about to get awkward. Of course this had to do with Trent. "Ask away."

"Would you mind giving me a peek at the rest of your

stuff? You know, the jewelry you're putting out tomorrow." Rachel gave her a sheepish smile.

"Um, I—"

"I'm really not being a pig." She rolled her eyes. "It's for Christmas presents. For Jamie and my other sister-in-law. Or I wouldn't ask."

Shelby was speechless. Was this Trent's doing? While she appreciated his good intentions, she would kill him.

Rachel sighed. "I'm sorry. Pretend I didn't open my big mouth."

"No. Wait." What if she was wrong about Trent? "I'm hesitating only because I don't have anything else. This is it."

Rachel glanced at the dozen or so pairs of earrings, the lone necklace that was left on the table. The other two tables had already been folded up and put away thirty minutes ago.

"Are you kidding?" Rachel seemed genuinely shocked. "You have nothing else. The fair runs two more days."

"I wasn't prepared," Shelby said, miserable and embarrassed. "I had no business taking up a booth when I didn't know a thing about this fair."

"Oh, no, it doesn't matter." Rachel waved away the concern. Nose wrinkled, and staring off, she gave the impression she was thinking hard. "This is your main business, right? How you make your living?"

"Now." Shelby nodded. "Yes."

"I have an idea. How about you hang onto whatever you have left here…I'll even loan you the pieces I bought. I'll get Jamie to do the same," she said, waving a hand as if it was a done deal. "So you can at least take orders and make the jewelry after the fair. What do you think?"

Stunned and seriously touched, Shelby gaped for a moment. "That you're brilliant," she said finally.

Rachel laughed. "We'll get along just fine." She held

out her bags. "Feel free to pass around the part about me being brilliant."

Her thank-you came out choked.

"Oh, Shelby." Rachel dropped the bags on the table and came around to give her a hug. "It's nothing. We're a small, friendly town. We help each other. Well, most of us do. I can think of a few people I would love to kick in the tush, but hey…"

Shelby laughed and blinked several times before she embarrassed herself. No tears had actually fallen and she wanted it to stay that way.

Rachel released her. "I'll talk to Jamie, but I'm sure she'll be on board. She's inside with Cole and my other two brothers. Maybe you'll meet them later. If not, someday."

Shelby nodded. "You really are brilliant."

"I know." Rachel grinned. "Don't look now but the kissing bandit's coming." She stepped back. "Trent's one of the good guys. I'm glad he's come home. And that he has you. I bet you and I will be friends."

Shelby just nodded. Her eyes still burned and if she tried to speak she'd be toast. Rachel was right. This was Trent's home. And Shelby was nothing but an interloper looking for an easy way out of her old life.

# 16

THE FAIR ENDED after three successful days. Shelby had seemed to enjoy herself, and hadn't minded a bit when he'd had to run home to take care of Griffin. Trent had made it a point to be there for the tear-down, but enough people had volunteered that he didn't feel guilty leaving early to get Shelby home. Poor woman was exhausted.

They weren't too far from the Eager Beaver. Neither of them had spoken in a while. Thinking she might've dozed off, he glanced over at her snuggled down in the passenger seat.

She had her whole body turned toward him, her cheek resting against the back of the seat. "I have a confession to make," she said.

He felt his gut clench. She hadn't been quite herself the past two days. He'd chalked it up to exhaustion. After a jarring silence, he took a curve in the road, then glanced back at her. She was yawning hugely. He smiled.

"You know that first day when I met Rachel and Jamie?" she said, and he nodded. "I thought you put them up to it."

Trent frowned. "Put them up to what?"

"Saying all those nice things about my jewelry. Buying all that they did."

"Why would I have done that?"

"Because you felt sorry for me. You knew I was worried my jewelry wasn't any good."

"Yeah, but I also knew that wasn't true. And that you'd see for yourself soon enough." He reached across the console for her hand. "Tell you the truth, I was a little worried. I knew people would snap up your stuff fast and then you'd be upset when you sold out."

Her hand felt cool and limp, and she didn't respond. Even though the road was tricky for a couple of miles, he had to take a quick look at her.

She blinked and turned her head.

"Shelby?"

"Careful. There's a deer up ahead on the right."

"I see her." He watched the doe hover at the side of the highway, then bound into the woods. He was more concerned with the suspicious glassiness in Shelby's eyes. And the fact that she'd pulled her hand away. "Something bothering you?"

"You mean other than I've been sleepwalking for two days and I have a ton of orders and no idea how I'll ever complete them before Christmas?"

"You will. I have faith in you."

She sniffled. Turned sharply to look out her window.

What the hell? He pulled the truck over to the shoulder and cut the engine.

"What are you doing?" She straightened, glanced at him, looked away and dabbed at her eye.

"Tell me what's wrong." He swore, if she said "nothing," he would lose it. He'd heard enough "nothings" from his ex to last him a damn lifetime.

"We're almost home. Can't we talk then?"

"We could."

"Okay." She glared at him. "You're not driving."

"I said we could, not that I agreed."

"Trent." Her shoulders slumped against the seat. "Please."

"Are you telling me nothing's wrong?"

"No. I'm telling you I want to get home. Before the first snowfall if possible. Please."

Trent started the engine. He let her be for the ten minutes it took to arrive at the Eager Beaver and park. But then she opened her door and jumped out so fast he wondered if she planned to dodge him all night. Fine. He wouldn't say another word.

Shit.

Mutt came running from behind Violet's trailer straight toward him. He stopped to scratch behind the dog's ears. "How are you doing, boy? Have you been taking care of those kittens and their mama?"

He barked and led Trent to the kitchen door.

Trent sighed. Animals were so much easier to understand than women.

He let Mutt in behind him, scooped kibble out of the bin and dumped it into his bowl. Without a single complaint or cross look Mutt chowed down. Didn't take much to make an animal happy, either, unlike women. Trent should've learned that lesson by now.

Irritated with himself for giving a damn, he walked through the house to see if Shelby had closed herself off in her room. Just as he got to the hall she stepped out of the bathroom.

"Was that…" He closed his eyes for a second. "Better?"

"Much," she said with a regal lift of her chin. "Thank you."

"You could've just told me."

"I could've." She tried keeping a straight face. "But I didn't."

He lunged for her and missed. Laughing, she did a taunting little shimmy and danced out of his reach.

"Okay. I see how you are. Now that you're a mini ty-coon you think you're too good for me."

She stopped and stared at him.

He expected her to laugh. Maybe flip him off. Or play along by sticking her nose in the air.

Trent never thought she'd burst into tears.

And damned if he knew what to do. He froze, a bunch of stuff flipping through his mind, afraid he'd make a wrong move and chase her off. He could only do one thing—trust his instincts.

He grabbed a box of tissue from the bathroom, then he pulled Shelby into his arms.

She cried louder.

Holy hell.

She didn't push him away, though, so he hugged her a little closer and rubbed her back, letting her cry with her face buried against his chest. He lightly kissed the top of her head, hoping she hadn't noticed. She might not like it at the moment, but he'd needed the small comfort.

Wanting Shelby to call the shots, he stayed quiet and completely still, even when Mutt barked at the door.

She drew back, pulled out half the tissues in the box, and kept her head bowed while she wiped her eyes and blew her nose. "We better let him out."

Mutt probably just wanted to go chase evening critters. But Trent went ahead and opened the door to give Shelby a moment. After that… Hell, he didn't know.

"Can I get you something?" he asked. "Water? A sand-wich? How about a beer?"

She gave him a watery smile and shook her head. "Thanks."

Realizing he was still wearing his hat he yanked it off and spun it around in his hands. "Guess you're just tired, huh?"

"I am," she said, "but that's not it." She cleared her throat. "Maybe I will have some water."

They both turned to the kitchen at the same time.

"I think I can manage," she said with a soft laugh. "May I get you anything? A beer?"

"I don't know. Will I need one?"

Her expression faltered. "I don't think so."

Goddamn it, he wanted to kick himself. What a jack-ass thing to say. He'd given her an out. It would've been easy for her to blame exhaustion. But she seemed willing to talk, and what did he do?

Halfway to the kitchen she turned around. His gut clenched. She walked back to him, got up on tiptoes and kissed him before continuing to the kitchen.

Shit. He really did want that beer. But he wouldn't follow her. "Shelby?"

"Got it." Less than a minute later she returned with water for her and a bottle for him.

"Thanks," he said, and twisted off the cap. "This is not a commentary on anything. I just feel like a beer."

"Got that, too." She smiled. "Let's sit on the couch for a change, huh?"

She sat first, in the middle, which helped him out. Hard for him to make a wrong move. His ex would've plastered herself to one corner and silently dared him to overstep. Hell, why had he been thinking of Dana lately? He wasn't even that pissed at her anymore. Setting his beer on the coffee table, he sat in his normal spot. Shelby inched a bit closer. The warmth flooding his chest made him a little tongue-tied, so he just smiled and put a loose arm behind her on the couch.

She shifted to face him and sighed. "Thank you," she said. "For helping me get the booth at the fair. For having faith in me. For liking my jewelry. For…putting up with me. I showed up out of the blue, turned your life upside down and you still—" Her voice caught. She took a quick sip, her gaze lowered. "I guess I'm just trying to say thanks for everything."

Part of him thought he should just keep his mouth shut. The other part had him scared to death she was working up to a goodbye. "You're tired," he said, taking her free hand in his. "Now isn't the time to make any big decisions if that's where you're going with this."

Her eyes widened in genuine surprise. "I'm not. I honestly just wanted to tell you how great you've been and how much it matters to me." She took another sip then put her glass on the coffee table. "It's been a long time since anyone has been in my corner. That's why I'm emotional. I just—"

He squeezed her hand, wanting to hold her. But something told him there was more to be said first. "You don't have to thank me. Look how supportive you've been of me. What you said about Moon and that last call. Hey, we're—" His throat closed some when she warily looked up. "We're friends." When the hell had that word become inadequate? She felt it, too, and yet what else were they if not friends. "That's what friends do. Support each other."

She nodded. "You're right," she said with a short laugh. "Who woulda thunk it, huh? That we'd ever reach across that blue duct tape and—"

Trent groaned. "Okay, not a shining moment. Can we forget about that?"

"Well, what about me?" She winced. "Coming out wrapped in just a towel."

"Oh, well, that's completely different. Feel free to do that anytime."

Shelby laughed. "See? You make me laugh. Before meeting you, do you know how long it had been since I really laughed, or felt like myself?" She sighed. "Of course you don't. The other night I was trying to remember and I honestly couldn't."

"Ah, Shelby…"

She leaned another inch closer. "I'm not done thanking you." He opened his mouth and she put a finger to his lips. "Rachel and Sadie and Jamie, I like them all so much and they seem to like me. One word from you about why I came here in the first place and they'd hate my guts. Things would've gotten too icky for me to stick around…"

"I would never have done that." His heart pounded. He should tell her right now how much he wanted her to stay. Call them friends, whatever. It didn't matter.

"I know." She touched his face. "You're a real sweetheart. Even when you pretended to be a meany there were a lot of tells that said otherwise. And now that I know a bit about your world, I'd say every one of your friends knows what a good man you are."

Trent wasn't very comfortable with all this. "I think you're being over-generous, but thank you." He brushed her cheek with the back of his hand. How easy it was to get lost in that beautiful smile of hers. He could stare at her lips forever.

Damn, he needed to say something. Fast. Shelby needed to hear how much he cared for her and wanted her to stay. Now. Once Violet showed them proof that the ranch was his, Shelby might think he was only being a softie by letting her stick around, that she was extra baggage.

He cleared his throat. "What I said about being friends—" Why was this so hard? "You know I care about you…right?"

Shelby nodded, but she was worrying that lush bottom lip of hers.

Hell, his getting all serious could chase her away. He had only known Shelby for a little over two weeks. His feelings for her were strong, stronger than was wise. For both their sakes, they should take whatever was happening between them slowly. He hoped this wasn't just a rebound thing…for both of them.

When she drew closer and kissed him, he went with his gut and pulled her onto his lap. They'd had a long, full weekend and were both tired. Now wasn't the time for words.

SHELBY CURLED UP in Trent's lap, soaking in his warmth and caring. She'd never had a friend like him before. In fact, she had a pretty strong feeling they were a lot more. Everything seemed better when his arms were around her.

He was so different from Donald; Trent made it hard to remember why she'd ever loved Donald.

Trent tilted her chin up. His lips brushed hers softly, back and forth in a gentle rhythm as he stroked her hair. Her eyes closed and with his hypnotizing touch, she felt the stress of the weekend fade away.

If she could just stay right where she was for the next ten hours or so...

She pulled away for just a few seconds, far enough to see the way he looked at her with his beautiful gray eyes. Oh, yeah. They were more than friends. When she found his lips again, she wasn't nearly as tender as he'd been. Neither was the way she held on to him. She wanted to stop the world. Right here in this perfect moment.

At first sight, she'd thought he was just a hot cowboy. A pretty damn rude hot cowboy. But even as he'd tried to bully her off the ranch, she'd seen enough to know he would never do anything to harm her. That his grouchy routine with Violet was just a ruse to let two stubborn people take care of each other.

His tongue slipped between her lips, and she was back in the present, in the safety of his arms. She needed to re-member everything. The soft groan he made when she fol-lowed his tongue back into his mouth. How fast he could make her heart pound while the rest of her was as relaxed as Mutt in front of the fireplace.

Making out with Trent should be included among the wonders of the world. Not that she wanted anyone else to prove her point. The thought of someone else kissing him...

She pulled back and met his gaze again. He seemed surprised, a little worried. It was nothing compared to how she felt.

"You okay?" he asked.

She nodded. "If I ask you to take me to bed, just to cuddle, would that be all right?"

His slow smile made her melt inside. "Anything," he said. He helped her up and they walked to his bedroom in no hurry. When they got there, he turned down the bedding, then took off Shelby's clothes. The whole time, she just smiled. Memorizing his gentle touch, his reverent looks. Pity she'd probably be asleep by the time he could join her.

She slipped between the cool sheets and lay on her side, both hands underneath her head as she watched him strip bare. He was mostly hard when he walked around to the other side, but all he did was scoot in back of her and tuck her in close. He made a perfect big spoon.

He cuddled like a champ, and yeah, there was no mistaking his condition. But when his hand moved down her tummy and snuck in between her thighs, he whispered, "Don't worry. This is all about you. All you have to do is close your eyes and enjoy. Okay?"

She nodded. No one had ever...

His talented fingers knew exactly what to do. The key was slow and steady. Circling her clit until she was moving her hips, breathing deeper. Clutching his arm and the bottom sheet as he patiently drove her nuts.

"Come on, baby," he said, kissing her shoulder. "That's it. Just let go."

She nearly tore the sheet as her climax started deep inside. Like swirling clouds about to become a tornado, all the ripples started coming together, swelling underneath his fingers.

"I've got you," he whispered. "I'm right here. Let go, honey. I've got you."

It hit her hard, not just between her legs, but all over. He held her as she trembled. Not just because of her orgasm, but because she completely believed him.

As soon as the quaking subsided, she turned to face him. He smiled, until she drew away and sat up.

"Where are you going?"

"Nowhere." She pushed at his shoulders and he fell back.

"No, Shelby, that's not what I was trying to—"

"I know." She swung a leg over his hips and straddled him. "This is what I want."

"You're tired."

"Shut up," she said and leaned down to kiss him. It took little to get him to respond.

While their tongues explored and mated, she reached between them. He was hard. Incredibly hard, the silky head smooth and moist. She firmed her grasp and slid down the length of him. His breath stuttered in her mouth. She only teased him for a few seconds before she grabbed a condom from the nightstand, sheathed him, then positioned him to enter her.

She sank down all the way and his moan filled the room. He cupped her breasts, his hands shaking as he gently kneaded. Rocking against him, she fought the stunning surge of pressure building in her own body.

"Ah, Shelby." He was gazing up at her, the tenderness in his face nearly her undoing.

She lifted slightly and came down harder.

He bucked up squeezing his eyes shut. "Take it slower," he whispered. "Please."

No, not this time. She wanted him to explode just as she had done.

It barely took any movement at all. She rocked once, twice, and they both trembled.

Froze.

He whispered her name the same instant she whispered his. She started to move again. In a matter of seconds the world shattered around them.

# 17

SHELBY STARED AT the bags littering her workroom and groaned. After digging through every one of them she still couldn't find the special wire cutters and polished hammer she'd bought in Kalispell yesterday. They weren't in her trunk, either. She'd checked. Twice. She really had to do something about organizing her work space.

"What's wrong?"

She looked up to find Trent leaning against the doorframe, a steaming mug in his hand and a telltale smile on his face. "Don't even—"

"What?"

"You think I don't know that smile by now? Please. We are both too busy to start having—"

He pushed off the doorframe and walked into the room, with an expression of faint amusement. "Go ahead and finish. Having what?"

Oh, he was going to make her insane. She met him partway, grabbed the front of his shirt and gently pulled him down so their lips were inches apart. "You're lucky you're holding that coffee."

"I can put it down."

Shelby laughed and gave him a quick kiss. "I really can't."

Trent chuckled. "Hey, I came in to get a refill and was minding my own business when I heard you shriek. I'm just here to investigate, ma'am. That's all."

"I don't think I shrieked." She sighed and, stepping back, glanced around the floor. "I really am an organized person. It's just— I'm glad for this room. It's wonderful. But I need to get better set up or I'll never fill all those orders in time. Jeez, what a nightmare."

"In time? You mean for Christmas?"

She shrugged. "I know some of the jewelry is for gifts."

"It's been only three days since the fair and this is Blackfoot Falls. You meet a deadline or do anything too quickly and everyone will start talking. By day two word will have spread that you're an alien."

"Fine. If people start hounding me about their orders, I'll send them to you."

He smiled. "Come here."

"See? I knew it." She couldn't help her own grin as she took the four steps back to him.

The kiss began light, a brush of lips, a tiny nip, a quick taste. As usual, within seconds they gave in to it. She wouldn't let them get carried away, though. Not so much because she was busy, but she knew Trent was rushing to beat winter, and he was tired from all the sheet-tangling lasting into the wee hours.

She broke the kiss. "We need to talk," she said, putting up a finger. "Not now. Later." The late nights really had to stop. It wasn't as if either of them were going anywhere…

A sudden painful awareness squeezed her chest. Ten days, Violet had said. Which meant D-day would be…

Shelby sucked in a deep breath. It was no wonder she couldn't hold on to the looming date she'd calculated a hundred times. The whole thing was stressing her out. It wasn't today and not tomorrow. No, wait. Maybe it was tomorrow. And she hadn't done anything about it. She'd thought about visiting Violet, but the woman had practically disappeared.

"A talk?" Trent pushed a hand through his adorably rumpled hair. "Am I gonna hate it?"

"Possibly." She gave him a deceptively bright smile. "For now I have to run into town since I can't seem to keep track of a darn thing." She swept a gaze over the ridiculous number of packages. "Need anything?"

He relaxed. "Condoms."

Yes, they had more to discuss than she'd thought initially. But no point in making him tense—

"What? Condoms?"

"Get the big box."

The Food Mart and Abe's Variety were the only two places she'd find them. "You couldn't have told me yesterday when I was in Kalispell?"

Trent laughed. She glared, and he only laughed harder.

"You're a sophisticated city woman. I didn't think you'd have a problem with—" he lowered his voice to a whisper "—*s-e-x*."

She blushed, but couldn't say why. Well, except…small town. No anonymity.

Pretty good reasons why she was a smidge embarrassed. "Fine." She scooped her purse off the floor. "I'll buy the biggest box they have."

"I was just teasing." He lowered his chin and gave her a contrite puppy-dog look. "We're okay until I go in to pick up my feed order on Friday."

"Nope. Already on my list. A supersize box. Just so long as you can live up to the order."

He laughed again, put an arm around her waist and planted a noisy kiss on her cheek. "Darlin', I'll do my best."

Trent had asked for the large box, she thought, smiling

all the way to her car. Look at her, making plans, looking forward to a future with Trent. Was she...falling in love? With the man who might lose his ranch, his home, because of her?

God, very scary thought.

Unfortunately, that didn't make it less true.

TRENT HAD JUST swapped out the rusty metal fence post for a sturdy cedar pole when he heard a car. It didn't sound like Violet's truck—he'd been praying she'd come home before Shelby so he could speak with her in private. No, this engine was smooth, the rich purr similar to Shelby's sedan.

He rounded the barn just as a black car pulled to a stop. A Mercedes? Sweat trickled down his forehead into his eye. Damn weather was being fickle. Yanking up his T-shirt, he blotted the sweat from his eye as he approached the sedan.

The driver had climbed out. A tall thirty-something man with dark blond hair was staring at Trent as if he was part of a freak show. He pulled down the hem of his shirt, grabbed his hat off the wheelbarrow and watched the stranger pan the house and stable with a critical frown.

"Afternoon," Trent said, setting the Stetson on his head and pulling down the rim against the sun. "Can I help you?" The second the words left his mouth he noticed the Colorado plate.

Shit.

"I'm not sure." The man checked his phone, glanced back toward the house. "Do you know Shelby Foster?"

"I do."

His faintly patronizing smile stuck in Trent's craw. "Is she here?"

"Nope."

"Do you know where she is?"

Trent was tempted to just say *yep*. "Who's asking?"

"Donald Williamson. Her fiancé."

"Huh. Sorry." Wiping his palm on his jeans, he walked around the hood with his grime-streaked hand extended. And thoroughly enjoyed watching Donald's look of disdain turn to dread. "I thought you two split up."

The man's gaze shot up to meet Trent's. He seemed barely mindful of Trent firmly pumping his hand. "Is that what Shelby told you?"

"She didn't tell me you were coming." Trent stood back, folding his arms across his chest, feet planted shoulder-width apart.

"She wouldn't have. It's a surprise." To give him credit, he didn't inspect the grime Trent left on his palm. "Would you mind me asking how you two know each other?"

He scratched his jaw, trying to act perplexed. This was tricky. Trent had no idea what she'd told the guy. Obviously she'd told him something, though, or he wouldn't be standing here making Trent sweat. The guy was good-looking, he supposed. Rich. And he'd come running after her. Women liked that shit.

Jesus. Trent wasn't feeling so smug all of a sudden. "Haven't you two talked since she's been here?"

"Once. Briefly."

Trent's gut knotted. Time to decide which road to take. The low road was looking mighty good. "We're friends. Old family friends. Our great-grandfathers knew each other."

"Ah." Donald seemed vaguely relieved. "And this is the Eager Beaver ranch?"

"Correct."

"How long has she been staying here?"

No. No way. He wouldn't discuss Shelby. "Tell you what… It's Donald, right?" Trent waited for the nod. "Why don't you come inside, have something cold to drink. She should be back at any minute."

Donald didn't look overjoyed with the suggestion. He brushed something off his tailored navy blue sports jacket, turned and glanced back at the road, probably hoping to see Shelby's car turn down the driveway, then said, "Thank you."

Waiting while Donald pressed his key fob and locked the Mercedes's doors, Trent held in a snort. "So, Donald," he said, clapping the guy on the back and steering him to the porch, "you like beer?"

SHELBY NEEDED TO be smarter about planning her trips to town. Now that she knew a few people, there was no such thing as dashing in and out of a store. Some of the folks in Blackfoot Falls liked to chitchat about absolutely nothing. For goodness' sake some of them already recognized her car.

It was sort of nice, so she wasn't really complaining. But it would be much nicer when she didn't have a gazillion orders to fill, or a giant box of condoms to buy. She just had to laugh as she turned down the driveway. This sure *wasn't* Kansas anymore.

She saw a black car and couldn't remember Trent mentioning that he was expecting company. As she got closer, and recognized the familiar Mercedes, her heart leaped into her throat. How was this possible? Donald couldn't know she was here. She'd spoken to him only once and had never said a word about the Eager Beaver, or Montana for that matter.

Her cell buzzed. She parked, read the text. It was Trent, warning her about Donald. A little late. Could mean he'd just arrived. God, she really hoped so.

She got out and went around to the passenger side for her packages. Her hands shook, so she hefted the bags into her arms. The stupid box of condoms was sitting right on top. She threw everything back on the seat, not caring that the contents spilled onto the floor. She drew in a deep breath and took only her purse with her.

Dammit. Dammit. Dammit.

How long had Donald been here? What were he and Trent talking about? How had Donald even known she was here? He had no right to track her down, much less show up without warning.

This was bad.

Okay, she needed to calm herself. Slow down her heart rate. Anger and nerves, not a good combination.

God, she wished she knew if they'd seen her. She lingered on the porch, away from the living room window, drawing in long deep breaths.

Finally, she opened the front door.

Trent was lounging in the recliner, his expression unreadable. Donald was sitting on the couch, leaning forward. Looking out of place in his sports jacket. Both men turned toward her.

Donald smiled, and got to his feet.

She closed the door behind her. "What are you doing here?" she asked, annoyed when he approached to kiss her cheek. No need to make a scene, she reminded herself. And stood still as a statute for the light peck.

He reached for her hand, but she moved it back. Too bad Trent couldn't see her reaction from where he sat. God, she hoped he didn't think she'd invited Donald.

"You haven't told me why you're here," she said, unsmiling. "Or how you found me."

"Shelby, honey, I think we should have this conversation in private, don't you?"

Frankly, she couldn't imagine that they had anything to say to each other, period. Her resentment and disappointment toward him had started to fade since leaving Denver. But showing up unannounced and uninvited? She was pissed all over again.

But she needn't be rude, or make Trent feel uncomfortable. That was the last thing she wanted to do. She gave Donald a stiff nod.

"Guess that's my cue to leave. I got a lot of work to do outside, anyway." Trent stood and stretched. "I offered Donald something to drink when he got here ten minutes ago. You might want to get him something now that he's had to listen to me go on about our families being friends for three generations."

"Four," she said without thinking. She wanted to kiss him for sliding in the heads-up. That was so like Trent. What a wonderful, caring man. She should kiss him. Right now. In front of God and Donald. "Thanks." She gave him a small smile. "I shouldn't be long."

With a slow nod and lingering look he walked past her to the door. "Nice meeting you, Donny."

"Yes, likewise." Donald's troubled eyes stayed on her. He waited until Trent had left and said, "What the hell's going on with you, Shelby?"

She huffed a laugh and evaded the hand he extended. "What the hell's going on? That's what I want to know. How did you find me?"

"Your mom. Between the two of us we figured out you must have come here."

Shelby did a quick mental replay of the two conversations she'd had with her mom. Montana might've been mentioned, but— It didn't matter. "That you had to figure out where I was should have been your first clue. Why on earth would you think you could just show up like this?"

"Because I love you," he said with a hint of impatience, a dash of arrogance.

"Donald…" She sighed, suddenly so drained she could weep. "Let's sit." She waited until he was reseated on the couch and then took the recliner. It was obvious he didn't like it. But she didn't particularly care. "Because you love me isn't enough. I hope that doesn't hurt your feelings, but it's true."

Donald stood up, and she recognized his frown and his pacing. He'd been all ready to sweep her off her feet, forgive her silly tantrum and win her back with his heart-felt plea. As if.

"Look," he said. "I know why you left, okay? I get that now. But you didn't even give me a second chance."

"A chance for what?"

"To convince you we deserve to try again." He stilled in front of her. "You have to admit we had a lot of good times together, Shel. And you've got your job just waiting for you. Along with a nice raise, of course."

"Of course."

"We'll start fresh." He pulled a familiar box from his jacket pocket. The diamond was an extraordinary three-carat round solitaire, nearly flawless, mounted on 18k white gold. And it could be hers, just for marrying Donald—right after she signed a document stating it would go back to the family if they should ever split up.

"Put that away, Donald," she said. "Please."

He sighed. "If we can't work it out, then okay. But we have to at least try," he said, gripping the velvet box in his hand. "I meant it. I do love you. I never stopped loving you."

It was her turn to stand. Aside from giving him a pop in the nose for showing up here without an invitation, she didn't want to hurt him. He'd grown up in a world of wealth and privilege and she was sure he had no idea why she would choose anything else. "You said you under-stood why I left."

He nodded, moving closer, but stopping before she had to rethink popping him. "I didn't understand how impor-tant your hobby was to you, all right? We can work around that. I swear. Besides," he said, lowering his voice as he touched her arm, "You shouldn't have to live in this god-forsaken place."

*Hobby?* He so didn't get it. He didn't get her. And he never would. Despite everything, it made her a little sad. Still, it was tempting to tell him to just go back home and lose her number and address. But she really couldn't. After signing over a quitclaim deed to Trent, it was possible that she wouldn't have a place to live, or a job. Trent was still recovering from his divorce. They hadn't even known each other for a whole month. And one county fair did not a successful business make.

Her and Donald? That was over. But if she had to work for his parents for a while, it wouldn't kill her.

Then again it might.

"Tell you what," she said, taking Donald's hand. "I'll think about it, okay?"

He looked slightly appeased. "I knew you'd be reasonable about this."

She didn't bother pointing out that she was only agreeing to think about it. "I won't take too long to make up my mind."

His sigh this time was one of relief. She felt somewhat guilty for giving him false hope because she honestly couldn't see them fixing anything. But he'd caught her off guard and that wasn't fair, either.

TRENT WANTED TO kick himself across three states. He'd known eavesdropping was a bad idea when he'd walked over to the side window. Though technically the window was on his list of chores. It needed new grout, which meant he could hear pretty much everything from the living room.

He couldn't see them, of course, which was the only part that worked in his favor. Because if he'd seen them kiss or do anything, he surely would've lost it.

As he crossed to the stable to disappear for a while, he cursed himself for being every kind of fool. He passed the stable and kept walking.

She was going to think about it. About going back to that rich bastard and his rich bastard family. Why wouldn't she? She'd have it made. And she wouldn't have to live in this "godforsaken place."

He kicked a bush and it didn't do him a damn bit of good, so he picked up the nearest rock he could find and threw it with all his might. He should go back to the stable, saddle up Solomon and ride until the sun went down. He wasn't about to go back to the house.

She was going to think about it.

How could she? When they made each other laugh, and she was proud of him and he was proud of her. She'd already made friends here, and her business was off to a flying start, so what had he done wrong?

Goddammit, how could she think about going back to Denver when he was gonna give her the ranch?

When he'd already fallen in love?

# 18

TRENT HAD CAUGHT a glimpse of Violet's rusted-out pickup turning off the driveway and felt equal parts relief and irritation. She was trying to sneak back and park on the other side of her double-wide before anyone saw her. The hell with that.

He headed toward her parking spot at a fast clip, slowed so she wouldn't see him between the barn and her trailer. Then as soon as it was safe, jogged the rest of the way. That's when he saw the rearview mirror was gone, and there was another dent in the front bumper. Fender benders twice in two months. She was damn lucky nothing worse had happened.

She'd barely shut off the engine when he opened her driver door.

"Where the hell have you been for two days? Dammit, you can't just take off like that, Violet."

She glared at him. "I can, and I did."

He scowled right back. "I swear to God I'm gonna make you carry a cell phone from now on."

"That'll be the damn day." With a snort, she stuck her pipe in her mouth. Normally he would've backed up. She wouldn't hesitate to blow smoke in his face if it served her purpose. "Move."

He made his disgust known with a grunt and stepped back. She wasn't as spry as she had been just a few months ago. It was hard watching her climb down so slowly. He had to convince her to quit driving. It wasn't safe.

"You have bags you want me to carry inside?"

"I carry my own things. You know that." She shouldered past him.

"Jesus," he muttered under his breath. "I have to worry about you. Worry about Shelby. My life has gone straight down the tubes."

Violet stopped, her face creased in a frown. "What about Shelby? Why are you fretting about her?"

He glanced at the house. She'd been working last he knew. Except it was becoming more and more obvious he didn't know jack shit. Ever since Donald had gone, the two of them had hardly spoken. She'd grabbed food and drink when she needed it, then gone right back to working. "Can we go inside?"

"Come on." She had a Food Mart bag in one hand, a legal-size envelope in the other and a worried look on her face.

He followed her up the steps to her porch, wondering if the deed to the Eager Beaver was in the envelope. Tomorrow was supposed to be the day of reckoning, which was something he needed to discuss with her.

Reaching around her frail body, he opened the door. She didn't object. Something else worrisome. He followed her inside, his gaze catching on the small wood-burning stove. "I left a stack of firewood for you in the back," he said absently.

Watching him closely, Violet set down the bag and envelope. "Well, go ahead and talk, seems you've got something you wanna get off your chest."

"I do. First, you're gonna be mad, but so be it. You can't drive anymore, Violet. You just can't. You can barely see over the wheel. And your eyes aren't so good. You've been lucky so far, and haven't hurt yourself or someone else, but luck can't hold out forever. Besides, even as ornery as you are, I don't think you want to worry me like you did these past two days."

With a leathery hand she gestured for him to sit. "Next."

Shocked, Trent stared at her a moment then took a seat.

"It's Shelby." Sighing, he rubbed his closed eyes. "I want her to have the Eager Beaver. I'll sign whatever it is I need to sign."

"Why would you do a damn fool thing like that?" she muttered. "And you think *I'm* senile."

He opened his eyes just as she lost a smile. "I never said you were senile." He groaned when she walked away. "We're not done. Where are you going?"

"To get you a beer, you damn cry baby."

"Okay." He slumped back. "Good. Thanks."

She brought two bottles out of the refrigerator and let him twist the caps off. They took swigs at the same time.

"Explain to me why you want to sign the ranch over," Violet said, settling into her plaid recliner.

"Shelby needs a place to call her own. A place that won't cost her an arm and a leg while she gets her business off the ground. She needs to feel independent. You of all people should understand." He looked at the big envelope she'd brought in. "I assume that's the deed. Just, she can't know I signed the ranch over to her. That's important."

Violet's narrowed eyes bore into him. She gulped some beer without taking her gaze off his face. "Ever consider that what she needs is you?"

"Come on, Violet, don't start meddling in that area. You know I'm recently divorced. And Shelby was engaged until a few weeks ago. She needs space, and time to think. We can't just— Look, I'm trying to do the right thing here."

"So?"

"So it's complicated. We don't even know each other all that well."

She snorted. "You know her well enough to hand over the Eager Beaver."

Trent clamped his mouth shut. Hard to argue that point. After another pull of beer, he said, "If I don't, I'm afraid she'll go back to Denver. To her old job. Maybe even marry her ex-fiancé." There. He'd voiced his biggest fear. The thought alone was killing him.

Violet frowned. "What would you do if she doesn't want you to stick around?"

His gut clenched at the possibility. "I don't know yet. But I have more options than she does."

"Good God in heaven. You've always been my favorite, Trent. Don't be a dummy." Violet shook her head. "Fretting over my poor eyesight, when you can't see what's plain as day."

"Dammit, Violet—"

"Go on. Get. I missed my nap." She pushed to her feet.

"You know what, why don't you just give me the paperwork, and I'll go down to the county office and make things official."

Violet smirked. "You got any idea how old that piece of paper is? It ain't in just your name." She sighed with disgust. "If you want the girl to have it, I'll take care of it." Her face softened. "But I'm telling you, it's not the Eager Beaver that'll keep her here."

Trent felt as if his feet were planted in cement. A few days ago, he might've believed that Shelby felt strongly enough about him to stay. But now, after he'd overheard her talk with her ex? Hell, she'd slept in her own room last night. If that wasn't a sign, he didn't know what was.

"Feel like going out for dinner?"

Shelby looked up at Trent standing in the doorway. He

must have just finished working outside and washed his face because his damp hair was slicked back. Smiling, she set aside her glue gun. "What brought this on?"

"What? I can't ask my favorite girl out on a date?"

She raised her brows. "Your favorite *girl*."

"I knew you'd like that."

She doubted she'd be able to eat. Her stomach was acting up, and she'd pricked her fingers a million times on stupid silver wire. She'd slept terribly, wanting badly to crawl into bed with Trent. But by the time she'd finished working it had been almost 2:00 a.m. and she hadn't wanted to wake him.

It wasn't enough that she was panicked about getting out her orders. Tomorrow was the *day*. And Violet had been AWOL. Shelby couldn't rest until she'd told the woman she wanted Trent to have the Eager Beaver.

"You're thinking about going back to Denver, aren't you?"

"What?"

"It's okay." Trent shrugged, as if he was commenting on the weather. "I mean, I'd understand. Not that you'd need my permission."

"You're right about that." It was about the only thing he was clued in to from where she sat.

"What I'm trying to say, and doing a very bad job of it, is that I wouldn't try and stop you."

Speechless, hurt to the bone, she could only stare at him. She'd been praying for a sign he wanted her to stay. She'd really thought…

Oh, God.

"Donald seems like an okay guy." He glanced at the mess she'd made of the room. "You wouldn't be working so hard for peanuts."

Money didn't mean anything to her. He knew that. "So, tonight is supposed to be a goodbye dinner?"

"No, Shelby." The mask of indifference slipped. He finally looked like himself again. For a few seconds, anyway. "No. You've been edgy all day. I figured— I thought maybe you were dreading having to tell— I don't know." He scrubbed at his face. "Guess I'm still tired."

She had been edgy, cursing under her breath every time she'd nicked herself or dropped the tweezers. So, okay, she could cut him some slack. Still, tired or not, she hated that he could look so okay with her leaving.

"How about sandwiches?" she said, and tried to smile. "I don't really want to go anywhere until Violet comes home. Aren't you worried? Does she do this often?"

"She's home," he said, his expression a mixture of caution and concern. "We already had a talk."

Her heart pounded so hard she jumped to her feet hoping to slow it down. "A talk?"

"Yeah." He eyed her warily. "About not taking off like that."

"I should go check on her." She tried to skirt him, but he caught her arm.

"She's fine, Shelby. I told her she shouldn't drive anymore so she's not in the best of moods."

"Oh, so now you know what's best for everybody, is that it?"

"Whoa." Frowning, he let go her arm. "You don't agree that Violet shouldn't be behind the wheel?"

Shelby swallowed. "Of course I agree, but don't think you know what's best for me. Because I can assure you, you're clueless." She tried to squeeze past him. "Absolutely clueless." She'd tossed and turned last night, thinking about Donald and Denver, and what would happen once she relinquished her rights to the Eager Beaver. How foolish she'd been to spend so much of her salary on the right clothes, the right car, trying to belong in Donald's world.

Now, her savings wouldn't take her far. It would be hard to turn down working for his family.

Just thinking that made her sick to her stomach. Dammit, no matter what happened she wouldn't return to Denver. She'd rather live in her car than settle for a man, or a job. In fact, she was done with settling for anything. She was better than that.

And if Trent didn't love her? She'd be fine. Okay, maybe not fine, but she'd survive. Right?

That last part made her a little shaky.

"Excuse me, please. I want to check on Violet."

"She's taking a nap," he said.

"How convenient."

Trent looked confused at first, and then uneasy as he stepped aside. "If I swear to you Violet's fine, will you leave it alone?" he asked quietly as she passed him.

Shelby froze. He knew. Violet had already told him the ranch was hers, and the first thing he'd said to her was about how he wouldn't stop her from going back to Donald? How could it be that after everything they'd been through, Trent hadn't changed at all? He still wanted her to go back where she'd come from so he could have his precious ranch.

It hit her hard. So hard, she could barely breathe. Trent was supposed to tell her he didn't care about who owned what. That all he wanted was for the two of them to be together. Instead, he wanted to pack her off to Denver so he could have the Eager Beaver to himself.

She nearly choked on a sob and hurried on through the house. No. She wouldn't cry. Not again. Not in front of him, or because of him. Why had he been so great the night after the fair? How could he have looked at her as if he cared…as if he might even love her back. It made this so much harder.

For a split second she thought about changing her mind.

But keeping the ranch would be spiteful and so not her. At heart Trent was a good man. One of the best she'd ever known. He only wanted to keep his home, continue with his new life. She understood that bone-deep need. God, how she understood. But dammit, she loved him. Which was turning out to be a huge mistake. One of many. But this one would be incredibly hard to get over.

She paused in the living room, looked toward the kitchen. Where was she going? She had no idea where she was headed. Oh, Violet.

Shelby stopped again in the kitchen. Filled a glass with water and downed half of it. When had her mouth gotten so dry? She drained the glass, set it in the sink. Pushed her hands through her hair as she composed herself on the way to the back door.

"Shelby, wait." Trent was standing at the doorway to the living room. "Come on, honey, can't we talk?"

"Don't—" She whirled around with a finger in the air. How dare he? "Do not call me that. Not now. Not ever."

His stricken expression faded, hardened. "Okay." He shoved his hands into his pockets, his mouth a firm thin line. "Got it."

This was the image of him she needed to keep in her head. And not cry, she told herself again. Crying would be bad. She still had to see Violet. Pack.

Oh, God.

She pulled open the screen door and almost trampled the poor woman.

Violet jerked back. "Where's the damn fire?"

Shelby glanced over her shoulder. Trent was still there. "Can we go to your trailer and talk?" she whispered.

"Nope." Violet pushed past her. She walked straight to the kitchen table and laid down an envelope. "We're talking right here. All of us."

Trent eyed her, his expression a warning. "You aren't going to do anything foolish now, are you, Violet?"

"Nah, I'll leave that to you. Being so good at it like you are."

He slowly walked to the table, looking pale under the kitchen light. "Violet, I'm begging you."

He looked scared, desperate and angry all at the same time. Shelby had never seen this expression on him before. Her stomach clenched painfully.

"Actually, Violet, I really need a minute alone with you," Shelby said in her most persuasive voice.

"Tough. Sit down. Both of you. I'm missing my nap and my TV shows so I ain't in a good mood."

Trent folded his arms across his chest, his mouth clamped tight. Shelby tried not to notice how his biceps bunched. Or that he still looked a bit scared. She did as Violet asked and took a seat. But Trent, he wasn't having it. He stayed right where he was.

Violet dragged a chair from the table and sat. "I'm only going to say this once—"

"Fine. I already know." Trent cut in, staring at Violet so hard it had to hurt. "Shelby owns the Eager Beaver."

"What? No." Shelby shot to her feet. "You do. Tell him, Violet." She silently pleaded with the woman, staring just as hard as Trent. She crouched next to Violet. "Tell him," she whispered, her eyes burning. She willed the tears to remain unshed. "Please."

Violet blinked back a suspicious sheen of moisture. "I don't have the stomach for all this nonsense. You both own it." She slapped a hand on the envelope. "And I got this here legal document to prove it."

"What?" Trent and Shelby said at the same time and gave each other quick glances, as if they were opponents in a ring.

"But you told me I owned the—" Trent plowed a hand through his hair. "Goddammit, Violet."

"Wait." Shelby rose. "You told me I owned the Eager Beaver."

"I know what I said." She looked from one to the other. "I ain't senile."

"You sure about that?" Trent muttered something else but Shelby couldn't hear it.

She was too angry with Violet. "Trent warned me about you, and I didn't listen. Do you have any idea what you've done?" Outwardly she tried to look calm, but her voice was shaking like crazy. "How your meddling—"

Suddenly Trent was behind her, pulling her back against his strong chest, whispering, "It's okay, honey. We'll straighten things out."

She spun out of his grip. "How are we going to work things out when you want to pack me up and send me back to Donald?"

"What? I never said—"

Violet got to her feet. "Be mad as polecats at me. Not each other," she said. "I was young when they named me trustee, just a foolish girl. Hell, I've outlived the lawyer who drew up the paperwork. Had to deal with his grandson who took over. Explaining to that young upstart what needed doing 'bout gave me a stroke. But now everything's put to right. Harold and Edgar shoulda—" Her voice cracked. "Your two great-granddaddies were too stubborn for their own damn good." Without looking at either of them, she slid the envelope across the table. "Here's the deed. Both Kimball and Foster names are on it. So, figure it out."

She turned and left the kitchen without another word.

"I have no idea what just happened," Shelby said.

Trent shrugged. "I'm clueless, remember?"

She looked down, not ready to admit to anything until she understood.

"One of the things I really, really love about you is that

you aren't afraid to talk," Shelby said, then raised her head and met his gaze.

"I haven't always been that way," he admitted without wavering. "But I'm trying." He quietly cleared his throat. "Shelby, I don't want you to go back to Denver. I honestly don't understand how you got that idea. Jesus, it's the last thing in the world I want."

"But you said if I decided to go back you wouldn't try to stop me."

"I did say that." Trent nodded once. "When Donald showed up and I thought you might still have feelings for him. I—I don't know. I wanted to kick his ass all the way back to Colorado."

He sighed. "You are a smart, capable woman and you know better than anyone what's best for you. Now, if you did decide to leave, I'd like to think I'd keep my word and let you go like a real gentleman. But the way I feel about you? There's no telling what I'd do to keep you."

She stared at him, shaking her head, stunned silent not by the words so much as the way he said them. Okay, so he hadn't used the *L* word. It came hard to some people. If he needed time, she was willing to wait. Because this was the man she'd dreamed about long before they'd met. So she'd be brave. Be the first to say it...

"Want to know what I really, really love about you?" he asked, his eyes dark with emotion.

She could only nod.

"Pretty near everything," he said, pulling her into his arms, where he kissed her for a very long time.

# Epilogue

*Eight months later*

LYING ON HER SIDE, Trent's warm, naked body pressed against her back, Shelby squinted blearily at the bedside clock. "Please tell me it's not seven thirty."

His arm tightened possessively around her. "It's not seven thirty," he murmured into her hair, then kissed the side of her neck.

"Oh, good." Smiling, she turned over. They both shifted so that her breasts pressed against his chest and they could look into each other's eyes. "You've been awake for a while," she said, feeling something hard nudging her tummy.

"Not too long." He brushed the hair away from her face and gave her that special smile reserved for her alone. "I have an idea."

"Which is…?"

"Let's take the day off."

"Really?" It was the middle of spring and they still had so much to do in the three weeks before the two horses he'd been hired to train arrived. "Are you sure you mean the whole day? Or were you thinking we should stay in bed awhile longer?" Just to make her point, she rubbed against his erection.

"Both." He scooped her into his arms and rolled over so that she was lying on top of him. "How about it?" he asked, leisurely stroking her back.

Shelby grinned. "What did you have in mind?"

"Now, I know you can guess the first part."

She laughed, and Trent joined in.

"So," she said, nudging him again right where it counted. "What's the second part?"

"We need to give Violet her present. She's gonna try to hide out in that old trailer of hers, so we'll need to double-team her."

"Once she learns she can watch *Duck Dynasty* on her new smartphone, she won't give us any grief."

"Of course she will." He chuckled. "Just not for too long. Okay, so after, we could go to Kalispell for corned beef hash at the Knead Cafe, then drop off your necklaces at the Noice, go by the hardware store, get married, see if we can get in for the sunset champagne deal at the Conrad—"

"Wait." Shelby sat up, the covers falling down around her waist, and his gaze dropped to her naked breasts. "What was that last thing?"

"The hardware store?"

She socked him in the arm.

Trent grinned, looking her in the eye again. "Okay, okay. I thought maybe you'd like to, you know, get married. But if you'd rather not—"

"Wait."

"Again?"

She flopped down next to him so they were eye to eye. "We don't have a license. Or a certified copy of your divorce decree."

He gave her an innocent look. "Well, to tell you the

truth, we have both of those… Hey, wait. How'd you know I needed a certified copy of my divorce decree?"

She just smiled, then wiggled against him until he growled and rolled her beneath his body, pinning her to the bed.

There was no place she'd rather be…

\* \* \* \* \*

*Hungry for more cowboys?*
*Check out THIS KISS, the next book*
*in Debbi Rawlins's popular*
**MADE IN MONTANA** *miniseries.*
*In stores September 2015.*

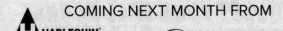

# REQUEST YOUR FREE BOOKS!
## 2 FREE NOVELS PLUS 2 FREE GIFTS!

**H HARLEQUIN®**

*Blaze®*

### red-hot reads!

**YES!** Please send me 2 FREE Harlequin® Blaze® novels and my 2 FREE gifts (gifts are worth about $10). After receiving them, if I don't wish to receive any more books, I can return the shipping statement marked "cancel." If I don't cancel, I will receive 4 brand-new novels every month and be billed just $4.74 per book in the U.S. or $5.21 per book in Canada. That's a savings of at least 14% off the cover price. It's quite a bargain. Shipping and handling is just 50¢ per book in the U.S. and 75¢ per book in Canada.* I understand that accepting the 2 free books and gifts places me under no obligation to buy anything. I can always return a shipment and cancel at any time. Even if I never buy another book, the two free books and gifts are mine to keep forever.

150/350 HDN GH2D

| Name | (PLEASE PRINT) | |
|---|---|---|

| Address | | Apt. # |
|---|---|---|

| City | State/Prov. | Zip/Postal Code |
|---|---|---|

Signature (if under 18, a parent or guardian must sign)

### Mail to the **Reader Service:**
**IN U.S.A.:** P.O. Box 1867, Buffalo, NY 14240-1867
**IN CANADA:** P.O. Box 609, Fort Erie, Ontario L2A 5X3

**Want to try two free books from another line?**
**Call 1-800-873-8635 or visit www.ReaderService.com.**

* Terms and prices subject to change without notice. Prices do not include applicable taxes. Sales tax applicable in N.Y. Canadian residents will be charged applicable taxes. Offer not valid in Quebec. This offer is limited to one order per household. Not valid for current subscribers to Harlequin Blaze books. All orders subject to credit approval. Credit or debit balances in a customer's account(s) may be offset by any other outstanding balance owed by or to the customer. Please allow 4 to 6 weeks for delivery. Offer available while quantities last.

**Your Privacy**—The Reader Service is committed to protecting your privacy. Our Privacy Policy is available online at www.ReaderService.com or upon request from the Reader Service.

We make a portion of our mailing list available to reputable third parties that offer products we believe may interest you. If you prefer that we not exchange your name with third parties, or if you wish to clarify or modify your communication preferences, please visit us at www.ReaderService.com/consumerchoice or write to us at Reader Service Preference Service, P.O. Box 9062, Buffalo, NY 14240-9062. Include your complete name and address.

HB15

SPECIAL EXCERPT FROM

*Nautical archaeologist Avery Walsh knows former
navy SEAL Knox McLemore will hate her when he learns
the truth. But she can't resist the heat between them!*

*Read on for a sneak preview of*
*IN TOO DEEP,*
*a SEALS OF FORTUNE novel by* Kira Sinclair.

"Keep looking at me that way and we're going to do something we'll both regret."

Avery jerked her gaze from Knox's bare chest to his eyes. "How am I looking at you?"

"Like you want to run that gorgeous mouth all over me."

"Hmm…maybe I do." She could hear her own words, a little slow, a little slurred.

"You're drunk, Doc."

Flopping back onto the sand, Avery propped her head against Knox's thigh.

She stared up at him, his head haloed by the black sky and twinkling stars. They both seemed so far away—Knox and the heavens.

"I've never gotten drunk and made bad decisions before," she said. "Was hoping we could make one together."

He made a sound, a cross between a laugh, a wheeze and a groan. "What kind of bad decision did you have in mind?"

"Oh, you know, giving in to the sexual tension that's been clawing at us since the day we met. But I guess you're not drunk enough yet to want me."

"Trust me when I say I don't have to be drunk to want you, Avery."

She made a scoffing sound. "You don't even like me."

Slowly, Knox smoothed his hand across her face, fingers gliding from cheekbone to forehead to chin.

"I like you just fine, Doc," he whispered, his voice gruff and smoky. The words spilled across her skin like warm honey.

He growled low in his throat. His palm landed on her belly, spreading wide and applying the slightest pressure. "I'm fighting to do the right thing."

"What if I don't want you to do the right thing?"

She felt the tremor in his hand, the commanding force weighing her down. If he stopped touching her she might float off into the night and never find her way back.

"I don't take advantage of women who are inebriated." His words were harsh, but his eyes glowed as they stared down at her. Devoured her.

Never in her life had she felt so...desired. And she wanted that. Wanted him.

"Please."

Avery was certain that in the morning she'd hate herself for that single word and how close she sounded to begging. But right now, she didn't care.

"Please," she whispered again, just to make sure he knew she meant it.

*Don't miss*
*IN TOO DEEP by Kira Sinclair,*
*available July 2015 wherever*
*Harlequin® Blaze® books and ebooks are sold.*

www.Harlequin.com

# Love the Harlequin book you just read?

Your opinion matters.

Review this book on your favorite
book site, review site, blog or your own
social media properties and share
your opinion with other readers!

**Be sure to connect with us at:**
Harlequin.com/Newsletters
Facebook.com/HarlequinBooks
Twitter.com/HarlequinBooks

# THE WORLD IS BETTER WITH
## Romance

Harlequin has everything from contemporary, passionate and heartwarming to suspenseful and inspirational stories.

Whatever your mood,
we have a romance just for you!

Connect with us to find your next great read, special offers and more.

f /HarlequinBooks

🐦 @HarlequinBooks

www.HarlequinBlog.com

www.Harlequin.com/Newsletters

H HARLEQUIN®

A Romance FOR EVERY MOOD™

www.Harlequin.com

SERIESHALOAD2015